SPIKE OF SWIFT RIVER

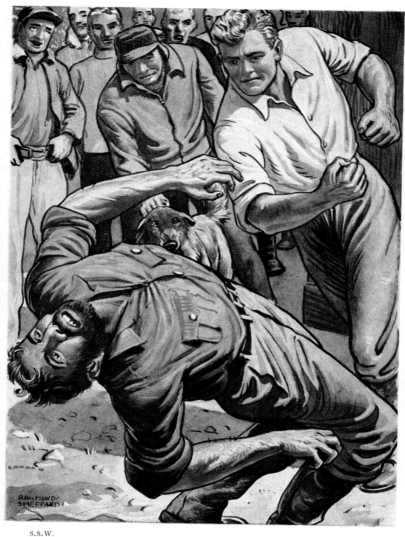

RAYMOND
SHEPPARD

S.S.W.

Dan's coiled right struck again, and McQuade's head jerked back.

(See page 109)

SPIKE
OF SWIFT RIVER

by
JACK O'BRIEN

Illustrated by KURT WIESE

COLLINS
LONDON AND GLASGOW

FIRST PRINTED IN THIS EDITION 1957
THIS IMPRESSION   1958

PRINTED AND MADE IN GREAT BRITAIN
BY WILLIAM COLLINS SONS AND CO. LTD.
LONDON AND GLASGOW

CONTENTS

CHAPTER   PAGE

  I. ALONE ON THE OPEN ROAD   7

  II. THEY MEET JERRY   24

  III. OUT OF THE WILD   41

  IV. THE WINNING OF SPIKE   69

  V. A FIGHT—AND A JOB   98

  VI. CRUISING THE BIG STICKS 120

  VII. TIMBER PIRATES   142

 VIII. SPRING DRIVE   161

  IX. SPIKE LEADS THE WAY   185

  X. PAID OFF   222

I

ALONE ON THE OPEN ROAD

POUNDING out of Pendleton four minutes behind scheduled running time, Number Six, eastbound special, swayed and rocked into the night.

The roar of the giant Mikado engine shattered the silences as the dazzling white beam of the headlight stabbed through the darkness like a searching finger. Smoke, blacker than the night itself, belched from the stubby smokestack to swirl back in tattered wisps around the ten big, lurching express cars which made up the train.

Inside the dimly lighted locomotive cab the noise was deafening. Steam sizzled angrily, steel banged against steel, loosely fitted connecting rods slapped and strained harshly. The acrid smell of oil and of damp, cloying steam was heavy in the air.

On the right-hand seat of the cab sat the engineer, a tense figure in blue denim. His eyes roved ceaselessly across the many dials gleaming on the boiler head, shifting up frequently to the rails where the bobbing white light fanned out upon the right of way. One of his hands hung loosely draped across the big reverse lever at his side; the other lay in his lap. Behind him stood the roadmaster, grim and tired looking, gripping the window frame as the cab rocked in ever-mounting speed.

Stripped to the waist, the fireman stood on the heaving steel floor-plates which bridged the coupling of engine to tender. With legs wide-spread and braced, he yanked the chain which lifted the latch of the fire-door. The door swung heavily open, and he stepped to his job of feeding coal to the hungry fire. Red tongues of flame licked out at him, their glare painting the man's naked, sweat-drenched body with a sheen of gold.

The straining body of the man swung rhythmically with loaded shovel from coal-pile to gaping fire-box, the muscles coiling and uncoiling beneath the smooth skin. Often he stood upright, gasping for breath, gaining strength to stoop and heave more coal.

No one shouted above that resonant din. There

was neither need nor time for conversation among these tense three.

The engineer's hand slipped up to the breast pocket of his overalls. His watch flipped open, flashing brightly in the unsteady overhead light. Peering over the blue-clad shoulder the roadmaster checked the time. The watch was returned to its pocket as the gloved hand reached for the throttle. Slowly, steadily, the lever was opened a few notches and the big engine seemed to leap ahead in a fresh burst of speed as the drive wheels bit into the steel rails. The roadmaster nodded and grunted his approval.

Back in the little red-painted guard's van, swaying like the tail of a whip as the engine put on a fresh burst of speed, the disgruntled brakeman sat in the "jigtop"— the upper bunk on the side of the van—peering ahead at the bobbing tops of the cars. Awakened from a warm bed by a jangling phone, he had been curtly ordered to take the second duty on the Chicago run. He had not had time to get breakfast, and he missed his morning cup of tea. He looked down to where the conductor, nursing a cold pipe, tried to hold a teapot on the small, potbellied stove. Only dregs were left, the brakeman thought bitterly and silently he cursed the engineer and his suicidal mania for speed.

"What's all the rush?" he inquired bitterly. "If we had wings on this thing, she'd fly."

The conductor squinted up and grinned wisely.

"Machine tools and dies."

"Machine tools?"

"Yeah, to catch a boat. They gotta be in New York in forty-eight hours."

"Why don't they fly 'em?"

"Too heavy . . . . Ouch!" he cried as part of the boiling water spilled over his hand when the train rounded a steep curve.

"Why all the cops?" the brakeman persisted.

"The guards?" The conductor sucked his burned hand. "I dunno exactly. Two of 'em in each car. Government stuff, I guess. Maybe afraid of sabotage. You can bet your bottom dollar on one thing —there ain't no hoboes ridin' Number Six to-night!"

But the brakeman would have been wrong to take the conductor's word for it for even as he spoke there was a "'bo" riding the blind baggage of the Special.

Clinging desperately to the leaping platform between tender and express car—the place known as the "blind baggage"—swayed a man, one arm hooked through the ladder on the back of the coal car, hanging on for dear life. He was a young man, certainly not over twenty-five, and he was dressed rather well for a hobo—or "had been." The white oxford shirt, tweed coat and grey flannel trousers had become soiled and worn in the short but violent journey, and his appearance to an observer was that of an out-of-luck gentleman furnishing a poor imitation of a bedraggled tramp.

Two days and two nights on the forbidden train had taken their toll in fatigue, too. Hours of dirt and smoke, of cinders and noise—noise more deafening it seemed than any he had ever heard—yet he dared not close his eyes for fear of falling asleep. That would have been fatal. He knew that if once he succumbed to the almost over-powering urge to sleep which flooded his body, he would be ground to meat beneath the churning wheels which screamed up at him from the darkness. His arm tightened about the ladder.

A flurry of cinders swirled around him. He blinked his eyes shut and buried his chin in the collar of his coat. Sometime during the last few days he had lost his cap, and the cinders settled in his hair and poured down the back of his neck. The bitter smoke burned his throat and choked his nostrils, nearly suffocating him. He burst into a spasm of coughing, gasping for breath as tears ran down his cheeks, streaking the soot which lay heavy on his skin.

The man was not aware that he was riding a prohibited "Special," although he had wondered about the number of men inspecting the train at each stop. Somehow, mostly by luck, waiting until the train had gathered headway before leaping aboard, he had been able to dodge the guards when-ever the train had stopped for a change of engine and crew or for water. All he was sure of was that never before in his life had he ridden so fast, and that the train was going in the direction he he wanted to travel.

Suddenly the frightening screech of the engine whistle split the air. The man on the "blind" shifted his position slightly and looked down. A golden shower of sparks flashed upwards from the wheels as the power was applied to the brake shoes. The train lurched and humped sickeningly, slackening for the water stop.

Instantly the man was alert. Another stop meant another search, and he would have to unload and hide by the roadbed till the train was under way again. Now not, though; the train was still moving too fast. He squinted his eyes free of the dirt and looked out into the night. Just blackness; no lights, no town; he could barely make out the dull forms of the telephone poles as they slipped by like grey ghosts. Then he blinked. The back of the tender and the ladder he was clutching were suddenly brilliantly lighted by a square shaft of light. He turned, squinting, to face a blue-uniformed figure in peaked cap standing legs astraddle in the doorway of the express car.

The guard whipped out a pistol and moved out to the platform, closing the door behind him. Jamming the thirty-eight into the rider's ribs, he shouted above the noise, "You're gettin off, 'bo. Now!"

The pressure of the gun against the man's side was eloquent. He moved to the edge of the platform and looked down. Although slowing somewhat the train still moved swiftly. The ground slipped by below like an endless black belt. The man hesitated, then turned back to the guard.

"Wait till she stops, can't you?"

The guard's answer was a violent poke in the ribs

with the muzzle of the gun. "I said, get off! Hit the dirt!"

Suddenly the guard changed tactics. Lifting the gun by the barrel, he smashed viciously at the rider's fingers gripping the ladder. The hand jerked away from the crushing blow just in time, and the man dropped down to the step on the side of the car. Swinging one leg out free from the train, he let go. He struck the ground running at a gallop, but the momentum was too great, and with a headlong dive he plunged into the gravel of the right-of-way and lay still.

The great train thundered past, coming at last to a jerky stop a mile down the road. Lights bobbed and flickered in the darkness as a thorough inspection was made. The clang of the water trough resounded metallically in the darkness, first as it was set in position and again as it was lifted away after the flush of its cooling liquid had filled the tender. A short blast of the whistle and the Special jolted into motion again.

For some time the crumpled figure along the rail embankment did not move. Far off in the night sounded the mournful wail of the whistle, echoing like a wolf call. The red lights of the guard's van twinkled brightly, then swept from view around the curve.

Finally Dan Kirk stirred, slowly, carefully at first, till he raised himself on his elbows. Then he rolled over on his back and lay staring at the flickering stars above. Reluctantly his hands started exploring, over face and shoulders, down over his body and thighs. Satisfied at last that he had escaped with nothing more serious than bruises and a violent shaking, he pulled himself to a sitting position. Then it was that a violent pain stabbed through his knee, and involuntarily he jerked his head and his lips narrowed into a painful grimace.

Once more the exploring hands reached down over thigh and knee, and Dan sighed with relief to discover that no bones were broken. He had sprained his knee, or pulled a tendon; at any rate the region around his knee was sore and painfully stiff, but he decided that a few days' rest would put him to rights again.

Holding his weak leg straight in front of him, Dan hunched himself till the small of his back rested against the rail. It was not very comfortable but at least the rail gave him some kind of support. He looked ruefully down the tracks in the direction from which the whistle sound came eerily through the darkness. With one hand he rumpled his hair to shake out the cinders while the other explored a coat pocket and found a crushed packet of cigarettes. Dan lit a cigarette, and leaned back against the rail and smoked.

It was a strange sensation sitting out there all alone in the silence of the night. His ears roared as though he were sitting along the seashore listening to the roar of the breakers, and his muscles twitched convulsively now that they were relieved of constant strain. The steady pressure of rushing air while he was on the train had created the impression of a strong wind, but now as he sat alone he noticed the stillness of the night. For a long time he rested, soothed by the silence. Finishing his smoke, he buried the stub in the gravel of the roadbed.

A smile twisted the corners of his mouth, and his white, even teeth gleamed in the darkness. "Nice busy spot they picked to drop me," he muttered, speaking aloud from force of habit. "Now if that blasted train was only stopping to pick up water, the tank can't be too far away."

Scrambling on all fours—or rather, on all threes—half rolling and half sliding, Dan slipped down the side of the roadbed. There was a ditch at the bottom; it was slightly muddy. "Good—there must be water up ahead." Sitting on the bank of the ditch Dan tried flexing his right leg. Each effort brought its answering stab of pain; the knee, nearly as rigid as an iron bar, would not bend at all, but on standing up he found that the leg would bear his weight.

Slowly, stopping every few minutes for a rest, Dan shuffled along the roadbed in the direction the train had gone. Once, leaning against a telephone pole, his hands touched a guy wire and, farther down, a wooden frame that had been built around the wire to protect it. The frame had been weakened by the blistering suns and the heavy rains, and with his free hand Dan managed to tear one board loose. This made an excellent walking stick; with its aid he could make better progress.

Dan had walked about half a mile when the

bulky outline of a water tank loomed ahead of him. Running his tongue over dried and cracked lips, he smiled in anticipation, and he was soon standing beneath the tank, listening to the cooling drip from the still-wet funnel. Water was also dripping from a spigot let into a standpipe head-high from the ground. Dan opened the spigot and let the tepid water pour down his dry throat until he thought his stomach would burst. Then he peeled off his clothes and stood beneath the spigot, shivering deliciously, for the water, though only lukewarm, felt ice-cold to his overheated skin. His body— lean, with muscled shoulders, sinewy forearms and clean narrow hips—gleamed ghost-like in the darkness. He kneaded the muscles of his leg as the water sluiced over his head, washing out the dust and dirt that had accumulated for two days. Rubbing himself dry with his hands, he struggled into his clothes and hobbled over to a nearby tool shed and sat down. Refreshed, but more tired than ever, he leaned back and closed his eyes.

"Phew!" he muttered. "This is the first time in three weeks I've had a chance to take it easy."

Three weeks! Had it actually been that long? It seemed as though only yesterday he had worked and planned and lived just as other people did. Now, as throbbing aches stabbed his worn frame and the dull pain from his torn muscles reached his brain, he felt as though he had been riding trains, dodging cops, and skulking, cold and wet, around railroad yards for years.

Yes, only three weeks ago he had been happy in

his lifelong dream of the perfect job—managing a lumber company. But in that short time the world had come tumbling about his ears. The failure of his company—his and his father's company—and the death of the older Mr. Kirk were blows hard to take; but harder than all was his feeling that it had all been so unnecessary. Why had the big interests suddenly decided to pull a squeeze play on Kirk and Son? Why? Why? It was a question that to dwell on too long left him slightly off balance. At such a time he knew only a deep and burning desire for revenge.

Dan tilted his head back against the wall; he was too weary to think. Slowly his chin dropped to his chest. Sleep came, and he lay as one drugged.

Limping painfully along in the darkness not far from the water tank, the shadowy figure of a big dog hobbled with great effort, his front left foot held awkwardly off the ground. Occasionally he stopped and sniffed the air as though the soft wind could give him his bearings. Then he continued his slow march until at last he came to the tank, where he lapped greedily at the little pool of muddy water beneath the spigot.

His thirst satisfied, the big dog stood still for a moment, an odd three-legged creature. Then, with the slightest hint of a whine, he hopped around behind the tool shanty and sank to the ground. Carefully he began to minister to his wounded foot with his tongue.

An unusual accident had befallen him. A splinter

of bark from a fallen red cedar had become lodged between the soft cushions of his paw. The bark, shaped like a fish scale, had cut with its razor-like edge deep into the flesh, and in the dog's frantic efforts to dislodge the wood he had broken it off close to the pad. Now the other half of it was buried, no part protruding to be grasped by the teeth.

With sucking, slobbering noises the dog worked on his injury. Suddenly he raised his head, sniffing the air. The ruff on his neck stood stiff. He turned his head slowly, while his nostrils quivered nervously. The man scent had reached him, and his hurt was forgotten as he dragged himself to a standing position, satisfied that he had found the direction from which it had come. Quietly he limped to the opposite shanty wall.

The dog's head came cautiously into view around the edge of the shack. He stood there hesitantly in the darkness, looking at the sleeping man and poised as if ready for flight.

For a long time he watched Dan. At last, annoyed by the stillness of the figure, he growled and limped off into the night. It was not long, however, before he returned, peering around the corner at the prone figure still slumped against the wall. Then, with head lowered inquisitively, he came forward until he stood beside Dan's upturned feet.

Carefully the long nose extended in sniffing exploration. Dan remained motionless, and the dog's investigation continued along the trouser leg, his body tense as he sniffed.

Dan stirred uneasily. Hurriedly the dog shuffled around the corner of the shed. Thunder sounded deep in his throat. But when Kirk had settled back to sleep, the dog rose and slowly moved over beside him. This time, after studying the sprawled figure for some minutes and satisfying himself as to its nature, he dropped down beside the stranger, settled himself, and flicked a red ribbon of tongue around his chops.

Lying there, head erect, he growled as if out of patience with a situation he could not entirely comprehend. But seeing that the unmoving figure had no intention of rousing and driving him off, the dog's head dropped to his feet and with quick bobbing motions he continued his efforts to ease the throb in his paw.

At times his head dropped between his paws and his eyes closed; then, as his quick ears caught some far cry, he raised his head, pricking up his ears and sniffed vaguely at the air and at the sleeping figure —only to drop his head again when he recognised that the cry signified no near danger.

The two slept and dozed for about four hours. Dan awakened first, easily and without effort. His eyes merely opened, his senses instantly alert as he lay motionless, adjusting himself to his surroundings. A heavy dew had fallen and his clothes felt sticky.

Then he saw the dog, now lying sound asleep at his feet. Curled into a golden bundle, he had his nose tucked into the brush of his tail. In the half-light, the damp coating on his smooth pelt made it glisten like metal. For some minutes Dan lay, studying his companion. The corners of his mouth creased in a grin. He was a fine dog, his colour a rich brownish tan, like the crust of well-baked bread. Across the part of his face which was visible, a strip of darker shade stretched like a bandage over nose and eyes. That and the tip of the tail were the only breaks in a coat of golden brown.

Dan concluded that he was a shepherd of some sort, but he was too young as yet to determine whether his parentage had been common or noble. And having concluded that much, Dan came back to his own troubles. His bad knee was still stiff, and now he tried to bring it back to life by flexing his leg.

Instantly the dog's head jerked upward. His body tensed and he made an effort to rise. His instinct was to jump up and run away, an instinct that for fleeting seconds was lost in a sudden confusion. Sprawled stiffly, with head thrown back and fore-legs braced, the dog uttered a low growl, and in his eyes there was an expression of uncertainty.

During those seconds of hesitation, the man studied the dog. Dan was struck particularly by the ever-changing expression in the dog's eyes. At times there was a soft film seemingly covering them; at times they rolled back wildly. It was as though the dog defied any movement on Dan's part. His body quivered, and the growl changed to a half-whimper. But Dan did not move. At last he spoke, keeping his voice low-pitched. Slowly he extended his hand.

"Here, boy. It was your idea; you picked me first. Come on now—it won't hurt you. Take a sniff and be friends."

The extended hand generated a fresh panic. Its appearance seemed to release the dog from the spell which had held him and he emitted a startled bark. To struggle to his feet and retreat all in the same motion was his general idea, but the result was disastrous. Unable to stand the pressure on his hurt paw, it crumpled beneath him, and he bounced sidewise for a few yards as if blown by a strong wind. With a final weak whine, he tumbled and fell into the dirt. He looked up at Kirk with a pleading expression, aware of the fact that he was helpless.

Dan rose quickly, and winced as he brought down his one hundred and eighty pounds on the weak knee. He hobbled over to where the dog lay, growling and trembling at his approach. Reaching over, Dan smoothed the sleek pelt and rumpled the thick fur behind the tent-like ears. "Take it easy, boy," he said quietly. The dog leaned his head back and looked at Dan with sorrowful brown eyes. "Yeah," Dan continued, "we know what's good for dogs, don't we, boy? you're going to be all right just as soon as you get used to having me around. We'll have to take it slow till we get better acquainted. Let's see that paw now. Easy, easy; it won't hurt."

As Kirk reached out for the sore foot, all the instinct and fear within the dog prompted him to fight. To rip at that hand, then get to safety; for heretofore man had always signified pain for him.

But he made no move to get away, nor did he slash out with sharp fangs. Deep growls rumbled a warning in his throat, his head lowered, his ears flattened, and his mouth stripped back over long white teeth in a threatening snarl. A gentle hand grasped his lifted paw just below the elbow while a calm voice soothed him. "Steady, boy. Steady."

Once the dog's jaws clamped down on Dan's wrist. Kirk was still. For some moments he remained there, motionless, holding the paw, and gradually the jaws relaxed and the growls grew less threatening.

Clumsily Dan kneeled on his left knee, and slowly he turned the paw in his hand. The visible edge of the sliver gleamed wickedly from the torn flesh. Easily, as though he were working on a child, Dan slipped open the small blade of his pocket knife, and before the quivering animal felt what had happened he had pinched the wood between blade and thumb and drawn it out.

"There. We'll wash that good now, old-timer," Dan muttered.

With handfuls of water Dan washed the cut thoroughly. Gently he squeezed the flesh of the paw till a little grey matter ran from the open wound, then he rinsed the paw again and wiped it with his handkerchief.

"That'll do for the time being. I'll fix it better as soon as we hit a stopping-off place," he promised with a reassuring pat.

The dog lay still. He had yipped a little when Dan squeezed the cut, but now he leaned back, paw lifted, and whined with his mouth closed while his eyes followed the movements of his benefactor. The feel of the man's hand comforted him. It was a new experience for the dog and his first fears were somewhat dispelled.

Dan grinned. "All over your scare now, eh? Somebody must have sure tanned your hide for you to be that scared." He patted the dog's hind-quarters affectionately and stood up.

"If you've hitched your star to me, you've got a long, tough road ahead of you, young fellow."

Dan hobbled over to the water tap and sluiced water over his head and face. After combing his fingers through his hair, and drying himself with the sleeve of his shirt, he retrieved his walking stick and started for the tracks.

"Come along," he called. "I'm hungry and we still have six bits. There must be some place around here where we can get a bit of chow. Where there's a water tank there's sure to be a town."

The dog hesitated for some seconds. At last, picking his way carefully, he struggled up the gravel slope to the tracks. Dan grinned.

"A hobo man and a hobo dog—and cripples at that. We make a good pair."

They started off down the right-of-way together.

II

THEY MEET JERRY

Now the sun had torn loose from its purple hangings along the horizon to ride free and beautiful, with a threat of heat, in the cloudless sky. The liquid call of the meadowlark rang out across the fields in all its startling beauty, while a warm breeze stirred the stiff grass beside the tinkling feeder stream.

As he walked along the raised roadbed, Dan Kirk occasionally looked back over his shoulder to see if the dog followed. His interest in the big animal was now thoroughly aroused. The dog's reluctance to make friends could be excused, perhaps, on the grounds that Dan was new to him, but Dan felt that something—something he could not quite understand—lay behind the dog's distrust. But even though the animal continued with his air of aloofness, there was evidence of his unwillingness to leave Kirk. Perhaps the miracle of the eased pain in the wounded paw was fresh in his mind as he hobbled some yards behind the man.

The dog had lived the full ten months of his life in and around the lonely little lumbering town of Swift River. There he had seen the light of day, he and three other cubs, snuggling close to the warmth of their mother's side. There he had first looked out upon the snow-drifted silences, bewildered and very much afraid of all the many moving things within the range of his dim vision, while the ever changing odours which had assailed his sensitive nostrils caused him to tremble in ecstasy. Bravely he had tried to focus his weak puppy eyes upon the world of man.

Before long he had been able to stagger big-footedly away from the slippery, straw-matted box, leading his more timid sisters into the fluffy snow. He had never forgotten that first venture abroad.

Stepping from the box, his feet had sunk into some soft, freezing stuff, mushy and white. Frightened, he had tumbled back, bowling over the other three pups in his haste.

More of the white stuff was drifting through the air, and particles of it had fallen on his pointed nose. He slapped his tongue around his jowls; the stuff was gone, but a strange biting sensation needled his mouth.

The mother dog quietly watched her offsprings' initiation to snow. Then she had moved out of the box and across the white ground. The pups had whimpered after for a moment before they too plunged determinedly into the drifts, threshing behind her like baby ploughs. Soon they were romping delightedly and without fear in the white fluff.

Then had come that dark, dreadful person they knew as master. The beatings they had all received from this strange creature whom they identified as man were still indelibly impressed upon the dog's consciousness.

But that was nothing as compared with the horror afterwards. The mother dog and her pups had been chained in their small pen and for days no one came near them. They had lapped at the drifted snow for something to slake their thirst, while their bodies grew leaner, their tempers more ragged, and even the mother went crazily around in circles while the pups, bewildered, whimpered and looked out on a bare world.

Then came men with sticks of fire. They had pointed one of these sticks at the dog's mother; it growled, only sharply, and the mother slumped over while the pups gave vent to piteous whines.

"Think any of 'em are worth savin'?" a gruff voice questioned.

"Naw, let's get rid of the lot."

He was frightened. He had attempted to lick his

mother's prostrate form, but a jerk on the chain fastened to his collar brought him to his haunches. That jerk was the means of setting him free, for it snapped the frayed leather band around his neck, and he stood there for a moment not realising his good luck. Then the voice spoke, impelling him to action, and as fast as his short legs would carry him he headed towards the safety of the woods. The fire stick spoke behind him, and in front snow spurted, but in a moment he had reached the welcome grey shadow of the tall trees.

Now a combat of emotions was being waged in the dog's consciousness. To him, heretofore, men had been untrustworthy. In all his brief life the only unhappiness he had ever known had been brought about by men. Consequently he had avoided them and had lived alone, free—if not happy—in his wanderings. Then why did he not return to the forest instead of trailing along behind this man? Why was it that he ignored the tantalising game smells that drifted in front of his nostrils? Why did he pass by, without a whimper, the fat, bright-eyed quail as she lay nestling in the tall grass by the feeder? Of course these thoughts did not take an orderly sequence in the dog's mind as they might have in that of a human being, but they did give rise to a conflict that left him puzzled and bewildered.

Dan stopped and called to him. The dog limped cautiously forward, stopped and growled. Dan waited, then called again. A few more steps the dog shifted forward, but still he could not bring himself to walk beside the man. Dan hesitated for a moment, then he turned and continued down the track.

Being ignored in so plain a manner was too much for the dog. In his reckoning it was for him to choose or refuse to go to Kirk. And for a mere man to turn his back on him with utter disregard—that hurt. Perhaps the dog felt that he had done enough condescending in consenting to go along behind the man, and that the man should return his confidence instead of rebuffing him. At any rate the dog's response to this slur was unlooked for. He found that although it was painful he could bear a trifle on the sore foot, and with this knowledge he went into action.

Bobbing clumsily up and down, yet moving with evidence of future strength and endurance, the dog rocked past Dan like a toy hobby-horse. He ran on ahead without once looking back, favouring the hurt foot by lifting it and holding it high every few steps. He ran for perhaps a hundred yards, then suddenly stopped and looked back, his expression plainly disclosing the fact that he had accomplished two important things by this act. First, he had succeeded in focusing attention upon himself once more, and secondly (this was the more important to the dog) he had once again ventured close to this man, thus vanquishing a fear that had lain within him for many months.

"So . . . you're not an old cripple after all," said Dan, recognising the dog's manœuvre. "And you think I'd better pay some attention to you, eh?

Okay, go right ahead. You're the actor and I'm the audience—but be careful you don't trip."

But the dog was indifferent to any remarks, complimentary or otherwise. He had won his point in gaining Dan's attention and he was not going to lose that advantage if he could help it. From then on for the next half-hour the dog gave the finest demonstration of unconcerned, carefully studied "showing off" that Dan had ever seen. Ambling along in the pleasant morning brightness and warmth, his leg feeling better now that it had soaked up some heat from the sun, Dan could not suppress his smiles as he watched the big animal's antics.

The dog behaved like a small boy displaying his full set of accomplishments. Keeping always in front of Dan, he would glance back quickly, then turn away, not wanting to be caught checking upon the man's attentiveness as he brought into parade the many skills he had developed by living alone in the woods.

Clumsily he flushed a bird in the marsh, stealing upon it with what was supposed to be speed and softness; but, because of the injured paw, the action was ludicrous to say the least. He jabbed his long jaws into the marsh in his efforts to come up with some fluttering prairie hen, and then looked quickly back at Dan for approval.

Dan called out his appreciation and the dog left that quest with an air of disinterest, hobbling on ahead as though to say, "That was nothing. Watch me this time."

The grasshoppers received special attention. Darting and chirruping angrily, they hopped around the big dog. The dog would stop, tilt his head to one side as he studied an insect on the ground then rear back and plunge, bringing his uninjured paw down swiftly, crushing the hapless insect with one blow. And always he would glance back hurriedly at Kirk, trotting just far enough ahead of him to ward off any familiarity.

Suddenly the dog stood still in the centre of the tracks. Dan drew nearer, watching him curiously. For a full minute the dog was motionless, his body tense, head lifted, nose quivering. He turned and limped back towards Kirk. He came close and allowed the man's hand to touch his matted fur. Kirk stopped, resting on his stick, and the dog moved on beyond him for about fifty feet and flopped down between the rails. His mouth dropped open in a sort of laughing manner, but he would not move despite Dan's calls

Dan was puzzled. Was the dog frightened or just wary? Ahead of them a trestle crossed the feeder, and beyond the trestle straight tracks stretched for a hundred yards or so, at which point the rails curved out of sight. All around them now were trees, with an open space behind where the roadbed widened to accommodate a siding. There was not a sound. Even the birds seemed to have ceased chattering.

Then Dan saw what it was that had disturbed the dog. A short figure suddenly stepped out from behind the trees where the tracks curved out of sight, and, alternately walking a short distance on top of the rail then on the sleepers, moved towards Dan and the dog.

Dan smiled. So the dog disliked human beings. He was more than ever puzzled on the dog's reasons for following him.

Dan whistled and started across the trestle. He looked back to where the dog, tongue hanging out, panting, lay stretched out on the sleepers between the rails. He made no move to join Dan. If the dog would not move till the person, whoever it was, had passed, then Dan decided he might as well wait too. He lowered himself to one of the cross beams, letting his feet hang down in the water.

The figure was closer now. Dan saw that it was a slim boy—about ten years old, he judged—dressed in blue overalls, blue working shirt, rubber sandals, and on the boy's head, perched at a jaunty angle, sat a notched felt cap, cut from the crown of an old hat. Over his shoulder he carried a bamboo fishing pole.

As the boy came nearer, Dan noticed that his hair was long and golden in colour and that fringes of it stuck out from behind the cap. Dan waved to him and spoke.

"Hiya, son."

"Hello." The boy had a high, piping voice. But the voice seemed to go with the sunburned, freckled skin.

The boy stopped, legs astraddle, in front of Dan and gravely looked him over.

"Been fishing?" Dan inquired.

The boy shook his head. "No—just going."

"What's running hereabout?"

"Pike mostly. Gosh," he said, his eyes lighting up as he noticed the dog stretched out on the sleepers, "how did you get Spike to come with you?"

"Spike?" Dan asked, puzzled. "Oh, you mean the dog? He did the picking, I guess. Spike . . . so that's his name? Who's he belong to?"

"No one that I know of. Rufe says he's an outlaw —steals from the town but lives in the woods. Nobody has ever been able to get near him before."

Dan was surprised at the boy's even, cultured tone of voice. Children were rarer up here in the North Woods, and schools rarer.

"What's your name, son?"

"Jerry, sir."

Dan flushed. The "sir" reminded him of his unshaven, tramplike appearance. He glanced down at his unpressed, dirty, torn clothes and smiled grimly.

"Live near here, Jerry?"

"Yes, sir. About a mile down the track. Swift River—it's a logging town." The boy's high voice held a note of pride.

Dan frowned at the mention of logging. All that was behind him now. Still . . . Dan was beginning to find himself as bewildered as Spike had been. By this time, had it not been for a minor accident, his being discovered on the Special, he would have been in Chicago. Even now he should be travelling east instead of west, but that was another accident—the dog, Spike.

"Many trains go by here?" he suddenly asked Jerry.

"I don't think so. One in the morning—it should be along pretty soon—and one in the evening. Then there are specials when the lumberjacks come."

Dan did not question the boy further. His eyes were focused on a clump of bushes downstream and there was a puzzled look in them. Things had happened too fast for Dan to take any real thought about what he was doing and what he intended to do. First had come the frenzied flight from the house that used to be his father's, then a hazy remembrance of fog-laden streets in San Francisco, railroad yards, freight trains, the damp air and the roar of the surf on the Oregon coast, and lastly the wild ride on the forbidden Special. It suddenly dawned on Dan that until the moment he awoke to find Spike huddled at his feet he had been fleeing. Fleeing from what? Fleeing from failure? No, not that. From the unwelcome but kindly meant pity of his friends now that Kirk and Son had fallen on evil days? No, few of his friends had been aware of their trouble, so tight-mouthed had Dan and his father been about business matters. He was fleeing something else—a nameless horror that the civilisation he had known could permit a fine man like his father to be cut down in the prime of his life, as coolly murdered as though he had been shot by an assassin. That was what rankled. Not the fact that he was poor and without employment; not the fact that his father's enemies had hounded him till he lost them by jumping the Special. But linked with his running away had been a running towards, too. The Special had been taking him towards Chicago, to where he could obtain revenge. And now he was stranded, miles from anywhere, as far from his revenge as before; and now, too, he was slightly bewildered as to the form this revenge would take.

The boy fidgeted, shifting from one foot to the other. Dan looked up, surprised. He had forgotten Jerry was there.

Dan smiled. "I've been wool-gathering. Okay, Jerry, thanks."

The boy edged sidewise and looked longingly up the track. "Well . . . I guess I'll go now. So long."

"Good luck!" Dan called out.

"Thank you, sir."

As Jerry crossed the trestle and started down the right of way, Spike lazily rose and got out of his way. The boy made a coaxing noise with his lips, but Spike, paying no attention, crossed the trestle and put his nose against Dan's shoulder.

"So, just as I'm getting comfortable you want to push off, eh, old fellow?"

Laboriously Dan gathered himself together and took a firm grip on his walking stick. The morning sun beat hotly on the heads of the trees waving above the right of way, but even the slight breeze could not dispel the sticky feeling of Dan's clothes. Dan was beginning to feel that an ice-cold glass of water would be more desirable than a hot cup of coffee when the rails began to make that peculiar vibrating sound that Dan recognised to be the rumble of an approaching train. Dan glanced over his shoulder. Down the tracks the boy had stopped to wave at him. A feeling of friendliness for the well-spoken lad swept over Dan; his had been the first welcome words he had heard since his father's death. Dan waved back.

It took a full minute for Dan to realise that there had been something very peculiar in the boy's wave. He turned around.

Yes, Jerry was waving. Dan looked closer. The boy had both hands high in the air and he was not even facing them! As Dan watched, Jerry fell face forward on the tracks, and clumsily, as though his body were too heavy for him, pushed himself erect again.

Then Dan realised what had happened. The boy had been walking on top of the rail, he had slipped, and now his foot was caught in the switch of the siding.

The vibrating of the rails became more pronounced.

"Come on," Dan called to Spike. "We've got to help Jerry."

Dan limped back towards the trestle as fast as he could manage with the stick and his stiff knee. He tried to run, but a sharp pain stabbed his thigh, his ankle twisted, and he started to fall. Dan checked himself with a muttered curse at his helplessness.

For a puzzled moment Spike, his ears cocked forward and a look of bewilderment in his eyes, stood and watched his benefactor limp down the track. Spike could not understand the reason for this sudden change of direction, but he felt that his place was with this man, so he limped down the track behind Dan.

Kirk prayed that the boy would have sense enough to loosen his shoe and slip out of it. What Dan feared most then happened. A wailing whistle broke the silence in a mournful, distant cry. Above the trees near the water tank a cloud of black smoke rose and hovered. The switch was only a hundred yards or so away, and once Dan could have made this distance in jig flat time. Not now though— not with the stiff knee. He broke into a run. He stumbled and nearly fell. He righted himself and ran again.

For a moment his attention shifted from his own agonised crawling to the boy up ahead. Jerry was stooping over now and Dan hoped he was un-fastening the laces of his sandal. But no. Jerry stood up. Once more flailing arms beat the air as the boy continued his frantic efforts to free himself.

Now the long black nozzle of a heavy freight engine slid out from behind a clump of trees in the distance. It had a sinister look. Dan trembled as he saw its long snout poke its sniffling way up the track, moving with deceptive slowness, for each moment now seemed an eternity.

Kirk shouted to the boy — shouted for him to unfasten his shoe and slip out. But somehow Jerry did not hear. And then Dan's ankle twisted; the stick cracked and slipped from his grasp and he fell flat on his face, scoring himself on the ragged cinders. The rails seemed to beat out a harmony of destructive rhythm as Dan lay there, his ear close to the source of sound. He tried to rise, but he succeeded only in hunching himself up on his elbows.

Spike had also broken into a run. When he saw his benefactor fall, he stopped short, approached carefully, and put his muzzle into Dan's hand.

"Go on, Spike. Go get him!"

This was a different way of speaking than the dog was used to. When Dan had spoken before he had consciously used a gentle tone so as not to frighten him. Spike was puzzled; he moved back a few feet.

"Go get him, Spike! Go get him!" Dan pointed ahead. This time the voice was urgent, but low because of its tone of despair.

Dan thrust out his arm in a pushing movement towards the dog. Spike shuffled a few feet, looked up the track and growled; but still he did not move appreciably.

The rumble of the approaching train grew louder.

Months later Dan was to remember this scene, and to realise then that it foreshadowed the kind of dog Spike was to become. In desperation and disillusion Spike had thrown off the yoke of man and had returned to the way of the wild; but in this moment of crisis it was not the way of the wild that guided him but the way of his more immediate ancestors—generations of proud Shepherds, who had found their justification for existence in being man's helper and a guardian of home and field, Shepherds whose prime qualities were instincts for obedience and responsibility. It was probably this instinct for man's companionship, even more than the miracle of the healed paw, that led the dog to trail behind this man, and yet even now Spike could not get over the strangeness of it. The problems of men were strange, too, and obedience was a master he had never been accustomed to. When Dan thrust out his arm at him, urging the dog to Jerry's side, Spike had drawn back and growled, bewildered because these new problems were too much for him.

Then, and this is the action that foreshadowed the kind of dog Spike was to become, he seemed all of a sudden to lose hesitation. His head cocked, he looked at Dan, and to Dan it was as though the dog was listening for some word of advice from his forefathers, then he gave vent to a loud, sharp bark and galloped up the track as fast as his wounded paw would allow him.

Dan saw Spike reach the boy, saw Jerry hold out his arms, then there was darkness on his horizon as the shuddering, grunting juggernaut slowly moved by. He thought the bouncing, heavily loaded cars would never pass, and the dirge of the trucks flicking over the joints in the rails beat out a promise of destruction. Had his leg not been crippled, Dan would have jumped the train and unloaded on the other side, but that was out of the question now. It took many terrifying seconds for the long guard's van to round the curve in the

tracks, and as its wheels finally clicked by a train-
man at the window ironically waved to Dan
The boy's limp body lay beside the roadbed, and
Spike was standing off some few feet narrowly
regarding him. The dog was afraid of man, but
not of trains, for he had often seen them flashing
by at night while he kept his lonely vigil on the
hillside.

Dan choked back a sob as he hobbled up. Then—
suddenly—Jerry's head was raised. The boy
gathered his legs under him and sat up, slowly
rubbing his eyes with the back of his sleeve.
Dan's sob became a grin then an honest laugh as
he realised what had happened. Spike had obeyed
his first order, and though it was too much to
expect that he would try to pull Jerry from the
switch, he had done nearly as well as that. He had
thrust his nose into Jerry's hands, and Jerry in his
desperation had grabbed at Spike's thick ruff.
Not liking this at all, Spike had pulled away, and
in moving away he had pulled Jerry with him—
pulled the boy right out of his shoe. Unwittingly
or not, Spike was a hero.

For a moment Dan stood over the boy, not knowing what to say. In his struggle to free himself
Jerry had lost his prized cap, and now long golden
hair tumbled down over his ears. Looking up into
Dan's face the boy suddenly started to cry. Without
hiding it, he stared at Dan while the tears ran down
his cheeks, making white tracks in the dirty skin.
Embarrassed, Dan turned away, and reaching
down, managed to extricate Jerry's sandal.

"It's all right, kid, forget it. Here's your shoe."
Dan held out the boy's sandal.

Without replying Jerry suddenly rose to his feet
and darted off down the side of the roadbed. His
thin body broke through the underbrush, and while
Dan, mouth agape, stood watching, he disappeared
into the brush. Spike stood off some ten feet, an
interested spectator.

"Well, I'll be . . . !" Dan muttered, turning to
Spike. "Did you ever see . . . Oh, well." Dan
pocketed the shoe and reached over and patted
Spike vigorously on the flanks. Somehow Spike
realised he had done the right thing. He suffered
the petting for a moment, then backed away and
sat down on the sleepers, unconcerned, and began
licking his paw.

"Come on, fellow," Dan addressed his new friend,
"let's get going."

III

OUT OF THE WILD

THEY had not gone very far beyond the trestle and the curve in the tracks, when Spike gave a repeat performance. He moved on behind Dan, flopped between the rails, and would not move despite Dan's calls.

Looking ahead, Dan noticed a shack or two by the tracks and farther up the hill the struggling outline of a village. He nodded and spoke aloud.

"So . . . that's how it is. No like people and no like the city, eh? You're a curious fellow."

He reached down and gave the dog's head a reassuring pat. "Well, you wait here while I go and investigate.   Maybe we can rustle up some grub."

Dan walked on, quickening his pace. The walking stick he had made from the dead limb suited his height better than the old one. Spike suffered his head to be patted, and when Dan left him he whimpered just once and a muffled bark sounded deep in his throat, but he did not move.

To the right of the track perhaps a half-mile distant grew tall stands of pine and spruce, spreading like vast regiments of green-clad soldiers across the rolling back country. Where the timber growth thinned, a river glistened boldly like polished steel, then swept in silent grandeur towards the railroad in the direction of the cluster of shanties ahead. Dan's eyes sparkled as he recognised unmistakable signs of lumbering. He spoke aloud. "Timber country! If that isn't a logging camp, I've never seen one. And why in the name of all that's holy would that kid be going somewhere else to fish with a perfectly good river in his front yard?"

Drawing nearer the shacks, Dan saw that most of them were boarded up. One or two, however, showed signs of being occupied. Smoke curled from their chimneys and brightly painted flower boxes formed a colourful base at the windows.

Close to the track stood an old boxcar firmly imbedded in cinders. It had been removed from its trucks and was secured to the ground, ostensibly to serve as a railroad station since the warped sign with SWIFT RIVER painted on it was nailed to the porch roof. A rickety wooden platform running along the front length of the car was bordered with wild flowers. As he drew closer to this makeshift station, Dan heard the sound of heavy feet thumping the floor inside, with an occasional burst of song. The next minute the sagging screen door flopped open, and a man stepped into view.

He was a rather ludicrous figure, well over six feet in height, thin and gawky. He seemed to be all elbows, knees, and feet. Unlaced shoes flopped up and down on his feet and his suspenders hung down around his hips. Thick grey underwear covered the upper part of his body. A towel was slung across his shoulders. He looked up and down the tracks, yawned, stretched his hands high overhead, and then caught sight of Dan. As he stood watching Dan approach, his eyes wide with astonishment, he looked for all the world like a skinny scarecrow.

Dan walked up and greeted him. "'Morning, mister. Any chance to buy a bite of breakfast?"

The man in the undershirt regarded him narrowly through sleep-drugged eyes. He scratched a thick mop of yellow hair before replying. "Buy breakfast! Most hoboes I've seen want to mooch their chow." With an irritable snort he walked to a bench near the end of the platform. Hooking the towel across the rail, he lifted a bucket and splashed water into a battered tin basin, then rolling back his sleeves he again addressed Dan. "I'm station-master here. Law enforcin' officer too. Name's Martin. Where d'ja come from?"

"Been travellin' quite a piece," was Kirk's answer. Leaning against the boxcar station, he continued, "I'll buy what food I need as long as the money lasts. After that I'll work for what I eat. How does that suit you?"

Another snort, and the unkempt blond head was lowered while Martin showered himself with handfuls of water. In the next few minutes great puffs of yellow suds foamed over the basin while grunting, gasping noises resembling those of a sea lion at play were the only sounds to disturb the early morning quiet.

At last the dripping face was lifted. Eyes screwed tightly shut, the skinny man's long arms groped for the towel. "Blast that soap," he muttered. "It's got enough lye in it to pickle a dozen railroad sleepers."

Dan stepped over, unhooked the towel, and dropped it across the man's outstretched arms. He smiled as he waited for the drying operation to be completed, an operation indulged in with such vigour that Kirk feared the skin might be removed in the process.

At last a shining face emerged from behind the towel and a slow, good-humoured twist appeared about the station-master's mouth. "Sure you can can eat here, son," he said. "How come you're hoofin' it around the country? You didn't let them catch you ridin' the Special, did'ja?"

"You mean that train last night?"

Martin nodded.

Dan grinned sheepishly. "I sure didn't know it

was a special. Yes, they unloaded me back near the water tank. Did she stop here?"

A contemptuous expression appeared on the station-master's face as he stood twisting a towel-covered finger in his ear. "*Stop* here! Did you say '*stop* here'? Man, she went through here so fast she'd like to take the roof off this shack. Rusty Davis and me'd been waiting for her. Rusty's a crabby old horse-thief workin' here in the summer as a watchman for Northern Lumber. Winter-times he's a bull cook up in the camps. Anyhow, me and Rusty's settin' here waitin', and pretty soon we hear a roar and Rusty yells, 'Here she comes,' and before we get to the door he says, 'There she goes,' and sure enough she's a mile down the track and me still tryin' to hold my hair on in the draught she set up."

Kirk laughed and the lanky Martin continued, looping the towel over his shoulders and reaching into his hip pocket to produce a wire comb. "Yes sir, that was the special all right and how the devil you stayed on is more than I can figger out. How d'ja ever get on in the first place? She was loaded with cops and ballin' the jack for all she's worth."

Replacing the comb, he squinted down the tracks. So great was his amazement that the eyes almost popped out of his head, and automatically a hand went up to scratch his yellow topknot. "Jumpin' catfish, will miracles never cease! Where d'ja pick up *him*?" Martin indicated Spike, who sat looking towards the shanty. The big dog had advanced to within perhaps a hundred feet of the station, driven by his desire to be with Dan as well as by a healthy appetite that was beginning to stir within him. There he sat, refusing to come any closer to the abode of man but very much concerned with what was taking place on the porch.

"He did the picking, not me," Kirk answered. "Found him lying beside me this morning when I woke up out near the water tank. Does he come from here?"

Martin nodded. "He belongs here, all right. They call him 'Spike.' But he don't stay around much. I knew that devil was on the prowl last night. Robbed me of a chunk of bacon.

"Half-breed owned him. He was a bad actor. He got to smugglin' liquor to the camps up the river, and first thing you know he gets himself bumped off. Never did find out who the guilty party was. Anyway, this breed had a Shepherd who threw a litter of four pups. In all the excitement over the killing, nobody remembered the pups, and they're practically crazy from not havin' any food, so the boys thought the kindest thing to do was to get rid of them. That one though—Spike there—got away and hid in the brush.

"Well, the funny thing was, a couple a months after that one of Hart's new men—Bart McQuade, and a tough customer, too—finds Spike there caught in a trap. He takes him home and pens him up and tries to tame him. But nobody ain't goin' to tame Spike, no sir. That dog took a hunk o' meat out of Bart's leg as big as my fist, and he had to let him go. Better look out for him. He's a thief and a killer."

"No one owns him now, then?" Dan asked.

"Nope. He's yours if you want him. But what in Sam Hill would you do with a dog while you're on the road—hey, where ya goin'?"

Dan stepped off the platform and walked down the track. "I'm going to get my dog," he called back over his shoulder. "We'll be right back for breakfast."

Martin watched him for a moment, then cupped his mouth with his hand and yelled, "He'll take your leg off, you blamed fool." As Dan did not stop, he shook his head and went inside. He dropped bacon on the skillet and muttered to himself, shaking his head. "Funny kind of hobo, that guy. I'll bet he's nearly starved, yet he goes back to pick up a no-account dog."

He poured more water into the bubbling coffee pot and continued his reflections. "Bet he ain't a 'bo at all—sure don't talk like one. Wish that danged Rusty'd get down here. I'm hungry as all get out."

But if Dan expected Spike to bow meekly to his wishes and follow him into camp, he was doomed to disappointment. One concession only did the dog make, and for this Dan was gratified. At his return Spike rose to his haunches and whined a greeting. He did not wag his tail, but shifted about in a sort of little dance, expressing his pleasure at the man's approach. He even permitted Dan to sit on the rail beside him and stroke his head while

Dan talked to him coaxingly. But all Dan's calls and pleadings were of no avail. Spike did follow Dan slowly along the tracks, warily watching the station all the time. But when he was opposite the shanty he flopped down between the rails once more and stayed there. Dan gave it up and returned to the depot.

Rusty, a small, bowlegged man, bald as an eagle, had arrived. Dressed in well-scrubbed overalls and a faded blue shirt, he gave the impression of a wiry fox terrier. He wore glasses and his sharp eyes flashed quickly over Dan. Then he noticed the dog, the set jaw muscles relaxed and his mouth widened to a grin, displaying an even row of teeth with a gap in the middle where three were broken halfway off. When Rusty smiled he looked like a rabbit. Calling to Martin, who was setting food on the table, he announced: "That's him, Rufe. That's Spike, the young devil." Turning to Dan he continued, "Rufe's been tryin' to catch him for a week. He just about wrecked the place last night. Found him out on the right-of-way, eh? Well, he comes of good stock, stranger. Should make a darn fine dog if you can tame him."

Martin spoke up. "Never tame him in a million years. That Spike's done nothin' but run wild ever since he was a little shaver. Just about robbed me out of house and home, but I'll forgive him if anybody can teach him manners."

"You don't have any food scraps I could give him, do you?" Dan asked. "Poor chap's probably hungry."

The two older men exchanged glances. Martin pointed to a box in the corner containing small pieces of meat and bits of bread. "Help yourself, son," he said. "You know by rights I shouldn't give the beggar a thing, the way he robs me. He eats like a horse, too. Well, I guess we won't run short. Help yourself."

Dan helped himself to a tin basin and loaded it heaping high with the food scraps. "I'll be right with you," Dan called as he stepped off the porch.

Spike's eyes eagerly followed the basin of food as Dan approached the right-of-way. All of Dan's attempts to woo the dog away from the track by means of the food were, however, unsuccessful. Spike sat there, his eyes wistfully following the food, flicking his tongue to catch the saliva dripping from his chops.

"Here, it's yours anyway, you old beggar," Dan said, placing the basin in front of the dog. He watched while Spike eagerly wolfed a mouthful, and then quickly glanced at Kirk out of the corner of his eye. Convinced that Spike would wait there, Dan now returned to the station.

Rufe set a frying pan back on the stove, flipped a dish towel over his shoulder, and pulled a rickety chair up to the table. "Come and get it or I'll throw it out," he threatened. The others followed his lead, sat down to platters of bacon and eggs, bread and coffee. The meal was eaten in silence.

In lumber camps, once the food is set upon the table, conversation is taboo. Mealtime in camp is the time for food, not talk. This may seem harsh to people in cities, used to leisurely lingering over their coffee, but if a hundred men in a small mess shanty were allowed freedom of speech there would be long-winded discussions and arguments with the resultant loss of time and delay in the preparation of other meals. The bull cook's chief job in camp is to roam between the tables during meals seeing that food platters are kept filled and that no one talks. If conversation—other than that necessary in requesting dishes to be passed— is indulged in, the offender is hustled from the room without ceremony.

So it was with these three, schooled in the way of the camps. They ate in silence, both Rusty and Martin noting with interest how easily Kirk fitted into the customs of the loggers. Dan drank his third cup of coffee and pushed back his chair. He picked up his dishes and stacked them on the make-shift sink. Rolling up his sleeves he went to work. The two older men exchanged glances and grins. Martin got up and brought out a big pan which he filled from a tea kettle, then Dan washed and the other two dried the dishes.

Later they sat smoking in the warm sun. Kirk leaned comfortably back against the wall of the station while Rusty and the station-master puffed on pipes. At last Dan broke the silence. "Quite a bit of country you've got around here. Who's logging upstream?"

Davis, stabbing the wooden boards with a wicked-looking jacknife, replied without looking up, "Northern Lumber."

"Oh, yes, I had forgotten Martin told me that."
Rusty peered at him over the edge of silver-
rimmed spectacles. "Want a job? You've been
in the bush before, haven't you?"

Dan flushed. He had been afraid of some question
like this. Well, there was no sense in trying to
back out of it. "Some," he said. "Why?"

For a few minutes the men were silent. Rusty
Davis continued to stab the planks while Martin
sat, arms folded, looking down along the shimmering ribbons of steel rails. Spike raised his head
from time to time to watch the three, but he made
no effort to leave his post on the tracks.

"I think maybe Hart could use a man," was
Rusty's comment at length. "Hart's camp boss
for Northern. Darned good man, too. He'll be
back here in a couple o' weeks. Better stick around."

"I'd like to," Dan said. Once the words were
out of his mouth he was quite surprised at himself.
Only three weeks ago he had said he would have
nothing more to do with logging, and only this
morning when the kid—Jerry—had said Swift
River was a logging town, Dan had felt that he
didn't give a continental if he never felt a peavey
in his hand again or listened to the stirring cry of
"Timber!" Well, he had said it now, and Dan was
not one to go back on his hunches. "Yes, I'd like
to," he said. "Meantime I've got to eat. What
about that?"

Rufe Martin seemed to come to life again. He
unfolded his arms and spoke up. "You can help
Rusty here. Rusty's messin' around faking at

keeping the camp gear in shape, but mostly he just sleeps and eats and argues with me. Never wins, though," he added, winking solemnly at Kirk.

Davis grinned at this and Martin turned to him. "What's the matter with the lad takin' the time-keeper's shanty till the crews come?"

"Don't see no objections," was the little man's reply. Rusty looked at Dan. "What's your name, son?"

"Dan is good enough for now, I guess."

Davis said nothing except to stab a new plank with the jacknife. Martin looked at Dan steadily for a full minute. His searching gaze told him many things, but chiefly that this slim, husky youngster was not the kind of person that ran away from things. He liked the clean, square line of Dan's jaw and the way the jet-black eyes held his unflinchingly yet seemed to keep him at his distance. No, Martin thought, there's nothing phoney here. If he says his name is Dan, then his name is Dan. At last he said, "Okay. We don't ask too many questions around here. . . . Well, Rusty, when you've finished smellin' up the country with that coke burner you're smokin', take Dan over and show him his new home. You can get your chow here with us, Dan—that is, if Rusty don't eat us out of grub before winter supplies come in."

Piloted by Davis, Dan inspected his new quarters. The house was nothing more than a log cabin, but the walls had been lined up to the rafters with clean smelling pine boards and there was a puncheon floor of solid white pine. The wall opposite the door was taken up with a huge stone fireplace instead of the usual pot-bellied iron stove. A cot, a table and two chairs, and a plain board desk stacked with dusty time reports were all the furniture the cabin boasted. Rusty left him and Dan went to work at once. Neither of the men had said a word about his limp and Dan found that the food or something had given him strength, so that now he did not mind the occasional stab of pain when he turned or moved too quickly. In an hour's time he had swept and scrubbed the floor, made a bed from the blankets that Rusty had got for him out of the warehouse, and hung a pair of faded red curtains that Martin had generously donated at the only window.

Dan was sitting on the edge of the cot, admiring his new home, when Rusty's bald head was poked in the open door.

"Come on in. How does it look?"

Rusty squinted admiringly around the little room. "Wait till the kid gets a load of them fancy curtains! She'll think us tough lumberjacks have gone sissy."

"Kid?" Dan questioned. "Say, that reminds me." He reached over to his coat hanging on back of a chair and took Jerry's sandal from the pocket. "I didn't see any women here, so I thought neither of you two bucks were married. Any other women in town?"

Rusty blushed—or at least the top of his head showed a little pinker than usual. "No, neither Rufe or me ever had the good sense to get hitched.

Rufe was all set to marry a widow in Boise once, but she up and ran away with a farmer who had a dozen kids. Why?"

"No other families in town?"

"Not now. No."

"That's funny." Still holding Jerry's shoe in his hand, Dan sat down on the edge of the bed and scratched his close-cropped dark head. You see, down the track a bit I came across a kid— young boy, about ten, I guess — he was going fishing. Said he came from Swift River and that his name was Jerry——"

"Jerry!" Rusty jumped off the chair he was sitting on as though it had suddenly erupted. "Boy, did you say? A skinny kid with yellow hair?"

"That's the one.   Who is he?"

"*He* nothing. She's a she. Jerry—Geraldine— Hart. Hart's daughter—he's camp boss. Don't tell me something's happened to her?"

"I'll be darned. High voice and long hair—I should have guessed it. Sit down, Rusty, take it easy, nothing's the matter."

Then Dan related the morning's occurrences to Davis, how Spike had refused to leave the track, how he had met Jerry and talked to her, how he had come to realise Jerry's plight, and then the girl's flight into the brush. When Dan got to the part in his narrative where he fell and he didn't think the boy could ever be saved, drops of sweat began to bead Rusty's forehead and his clenched hands showed his tenseness. Dan emphasised Spike's part in the rescue to the detriment of his own.

"That's why I can't figure why he's so backward in coming into town. He seemed to know what to do then. Of course it may have only been an accident, still . . ."

Rusty let out a long whistle that sounded like a sigh. "Boy, that dog can steal food from me for the rest of his life. If anything had ever happened to Jerry I don't know what I'd done. She's been comin' here ever since she was knee-high to a grasshopper. Stays here a month with me before Hart comes up with his crews. Hart's wife sends her to one of them fancy schools in the winter, but Hart figures a month up here's good for her. The kid likes it—regular tomboy. 'Course I don't know anything about kids—girls especially—so she does just as she darn pleases. . . . Say, do you think we ought to go look for her? Maybe——"

"No," Dan interrupted. "I wouldn't. It all seems simple now. I couldn't figure a boy running away. A girl, yes—particularly a tomboy. Her pride would be hurt. No, she'll come wandering in later on, in all probability as mad as all get out, especially at me. I'd just sit still. She'll come home."

Rusty scratched his head, a deep furrow wedging his brow. "I don't know. I guess I'd better see what Rufe says."

"It's just as Dan says," Martin concluded, brandishing a flour sifter in front of Rusty's puzzled face. "Leave her alone. Put that there rubber shoe back in her room and don't say a thing. I

guess Dan knows more about kids than us old
duffers do, him bein' young and all. . . . What
do you know about that dog? Seems as though
he deserves a good steak instead of them food scraps
Dan gave him. Come to think of it, I bet Dan
had more to do with savin' the kid than he lets on.
I told you I liked that lad's face."

"Unh-huh," Rusty assented, still scratching his
bald pate dubiously. "It's beyond me. Still, if
that's what you say——"

"That's right. Leave her alone. It's modern
psy—psycog—well, it's the way to treat kids now-
adays. Besides she's a young lady now, and young
ladies don't like bein' dressed down by ignorant
old codgers like you and me."

Rusty snorted at this last observation. If anyone
could see Jerry in her old blue overalls they wouldn't
think she was a young lady—why, even Dan took
her for a boy. He snorted again, more contemp-
tuously this time, and left the station to pursue
his duties, such as they were.

Dan finished putting some clothes nails on the
walls of the cabin and tossed aside the hammer to
rest his leg a moment. He was in a good humour,
still chuckling over the fact that he had been mis-
taken Jerry for a boy. You couldn't blame her
though, he thought; up here in the North Woods a
fancy handle like Geraldine was a distinct handicap.
It was lucky that everything had turned out the
way it did. Now that he knew Rusty and Rufe,
and felt the respect in their voices when they spoke

of Hart, Dan realised more fully, with a sinking sensation in the pit of his stomach, how near a tragedy Jerry's escape had been.

His conjectures were interrupted by the appearance of a sleek, tan head emerging around the edge of the door, followed slowly by Spike's shaggy shoulders. The big dog appeared uncertain of his movements. He wore a guilty expression, and his ears twitched as various outside noises came to his attention, and his head swung back over his shoulder as he checked on these noises. A funny little guttural noise escaped from his half-open mouth.

"Come on in—look us over," Dan said, grinning at the intruder. "This is where we're going to live if it meets your majesty's approval." Dan sat still on the edge of the cot and submitted to Spike's study of him.

Over at the station Martin banged a pan against the porch railing. Instantly the dog crouched, tense and quivering, and turned towards the door, looking in the direction from which the sound had come. Dan went on talking to him. "Come on in, boy. Nothing's going to hurt you. Come here and get acquainted. Then I'll take another look at that paw."

Patiently Dan coaxed the dog until at last Spike stood beside him, permitting Dan to smooth the short hair on his slender sides and ruffle his thick neck fur. With the other hand Dan caressed the hollow behind the dog's upright, pointed ears. This last operation seemed to please him. This was a new sensation for Spike, this warm, glowing, tingling feeling, and impatiently he nosed Kirk to continue whenever the hand dropped. But even though he enjoyed Dan's petting and to a large extent had overcome his reluctance to venture close to the little village, Spike still showed little or no demonstration of friendliness, retaining the aloofness which had been apparent from the first. Gradually his curiosity regarding Dan was overcoming his timidity. Moving nearer him of his own free will was the only sign the dog gave of his growing confidence. At last he turned away and limped to the door, glancing back over his shoulder as if asking Dan to follow him. Kirk followed the dog outside and walked towards the station, but here Spike seemingly had risked enough in his first venture indoors, for he circled the stationmaster's cabin.

Dan let him go and went inside. "Do you have any hot water, Martin," he asked.

"Yeah, sure. Why?"

"Spike ran a splinter in his paw—I guess that's why he came hanging around in the first place. I got it out, but I ought to wash the paw good and clean the cut before it festers."

Martin went to a cupboard over the stove. He took out a small, shiny tube. "Here's some salve," he said. "Like as not he'll lick it off, but it's healin'. Help yourself to the hot water—it's in the tea kettle. Ain't nothin' too good for that fellow after what he did for Jerry. Maybe I ought to cut him up a good hunk of steak."

Dan laughed. "After the way he's robbed you?

Besides, one meal a day is enough for any dog, even if he is a hero."

Spike had resumed his position between the tracks in the front of the station. He struggled to his haunches as he saw Dan approach, precariously balancing the basin filled with hot water. When he reached for the hurt paw, Spike lifted it and put it in Dan's hands The dog bent over and sniffed, just as though he were curious as to Dan's medical methods as Dan first washed the nasty cut, then put on two or three layers of the salve. Spike dropped the paw to the ground, then hastily lifted it again, sniffed, looked up at Dan and growled. "What's the matter," he asked, "doesn't it smell good?" He rumpled the big head and stood up. "Things are sure going to be different here now. I shouldn't be a bit surprised if Rusty or Rufe adopted you."

Spike sat watching Dan till he entered the station-master's cabin. Then he hobbled over to the river, splashed around for a few minutes, drank deeply, and returned to his station between the tracks.

It was five o'clock before Jerry returned to Swift River. She came down the logging road from the north, padding noiselessly with bare feet in the dust of the rut-lined road. Her overalls were rolled up to her knees and her legs were covered with the fine brown dirt. Somewhere she had stopped to wash her face; in the dull afternoon light it shone like a well-polished Grimes Golden apple. A thin strip of leather was tied around her head, holding the long hair in place.

Approaching the back of Martin's cabin, Jerry picked up a stone and threw it at the galvanized refuse can. The metal pinged loudly in the quietness that had settled down on Swift River. She made an unnecessary amount of noise going up the steps and slammed the screen door behind her.

Martin, yawning and stretching, came out of the front room that he called his office. His eyes brightened when they lighted on the five gleaming silver-grey fish on the kitchen table.

"Hmn, fish for supper! Just in time, too. Been out kinda long, ain't you?" Martin asked, a twinkle in his eye.

"I guess so. It was so warm I took a nap." Jerry's eyes avoided Martin's as she walked around the kitchen, picking things up and putting them down again. Finally she poured herself a drink of water.

"Forget your shoes?" Martin asked, nodding toward Jerry's dust-stained legs and feet.

She shook her head, her eyes large above the glass of water. "I like the feel of the dirt between my toes, don't you?" For the first time she looked squarely at Martin, and there was a sparkle in her violet-blue eyes. "Can't say that I do. Leastwise it's been thirty years since I tried it." He chuckled. "I remember when I was a kid I used to warm my feet in the grass where the cow had slept. Sure felt good on frosty mornings . . . . I'll clean these now. Go on home and wash up—supper in an hour."

Jerry's whole attitude had changed. She made a spring for the door and carefully closed it behind her.

"And, remember," Martin yelled, going to the screen door, "you'd better wear your high shoes when you go out in the brush. Never can tell when you'll meet a rattler."

Chuckling, he turned back into the room. "She won't be so anxious to go traipsin' off again. Glad nothin' happened to her, though. . . ."

When the dishes were washed, Jerry and the three men trooped outdoors to the porch. Rufe and Rusty were true to their word—neither of them said a thing to Jerry about the morning's accident. For once she forgot her finishing school manners, when Rusty introduced Dan to her in a very formal manner. She stuttered, blushed a charming pink to the roots of her hair, then turned away to the stove, busying herself with the pots and pans. During the meal she spoke scarcely a word and kept her eyes focused on her plate, but neither of the older men acted as though this was anything out of the ordinary. She washed the dishes, Dan, and Rusty dried, while Martin superintended, putting things away in their accustomed places.

Outside the air was hazy and golden as the sun, a molten red, skirted the top of the trees. The ground seemed purple and Spike was only an indistinct shadow where he lay between the still, shimmering rails. Before he had his own supper, Dan had taken him another bowl of scraps, which

Spike had eaten with complete relish, even licking the last crumb off Dan's hand.

Rusty commented on the dog's unusual behaviour. "You sure have won a pal, Dan. Looks like that fellow ain't goin' to let you out of his sight."

"Not as long as I feed him, anyway," Dan said.

"I dunno," said Martin reflectively. "I feel kinda sorry for him."

"Sorry? Why?"

"Well, he got a raw deal when he was a youngster and had to leg it off into the woods all by himself. Oh, he's done okay up to now, but sometimes I think he must get pretty lonesome out there. Must get hungry when there ain't any game in the bush." He paused a moment before continuing. "I'm sort of skeered of him, too. He ain't natural."

Kirk grinned. "Why do you say that?"

Rufe squirmed around until he fetched a plug of tobacco from his hip pocket. Deliberately he shaved it into his palm, stuffed his pipe, and lit it before answering. Sensing that Martin was about to tell a story, Jerry dropped the torch she was attempting to repair and moved down on the steps where she could hear more easily. When the pipe was drawing to his satisfaction, Martin replied, "Ever think much on this stuff about dogs havin' an unnatural sense towards people—or death?"

Dan looked quickly at the speaker, then at Rusty. The caretaker sat as usual, stabbing the planks with his jackknife.

"Don't think I ever did," Kirk admitted. "I have heard of dogs doing some unusual things."

"Unusual is right." Martin removed his pipe and pointed it towards Spike. "Take that feller there. He pulled off the dangdest thing I ever heard tell of. I told you I was skeered of him. Well, not exactly, but these things I'm goin' to tell you have set me thinkin'. You'll do some thinkin' too when you hear it."

The station-master stopped to stuff a calloused finger into the charred pipe bowl. Rusty fished into his vest pocket for a plug of chewing tobacco. Jerry squirmed into a more comfortable position while Dan took advantage of the opportunity to roll down his sleeves, for the air was chilly.

"That dog must be near a year old, eh, Rusty?" Martin continued.

Rusty nodded. "About that, I'd say. He took off for the tall timber right at the beginnin' of the season. Must've been easy three, four months old then."

Rufe nodded and picked up the story. "That's about right. Now, then, in all those months do you know how many times he's come back here to Swift River?"

Dan shook his head and the old man leaned over and tapped his knee. "Twice. Just twice. Mind now, I'm not sayin' he wasn't hangin' around the settlement more than that. What I do say is that from the day he beat it off into the woods until now, he was only *seen* twice in all that time. And do you know when it was he came back?"

Dan again shook his head and the station-master lowered his voice in deference to the importance of his statement. "Mike Swanson, one of the jacks at Number four camp, got his leg looped in a chain while he was top loadin'. They rushed him down here and Doc Carroll did what he could but it weren't much good. I was standing outside the shanty to get a breath of air when all of a sudden there was the most gosh-awful yell I've ever heard. It made any wolf call like Jerry's here seem like singin'. The hair on my neck stood right up and the skin on my arms got all rough and bumpy-like. Then it sounded again and I looked over to the edge of the clearin'. There was Spike standin' with his nose pointed at the moon, never a muscle movin'. He'd finished the last yell, but he must've stood there for a full minute. When he saw me watchin' him, he dropped his head and trotted off into the brush.

"When I got over feelin' queer I went inside. Swanson had died about ten minutes before."

Dan had been impressed by Rufe's story. His mouth felt dry, as it always did when he had been reading a good story. "There have been many tales like that about dogs, Martin. From what I understand, the only thing the dog's cry signifies is that he wants a mate. As to the time, that was probably just an accident."

"Accident nothing! That's rot. Listen to this, then. About six months ago a husky teamster got drunk and went through the ice. They fished him out and lugged him down to the Doc's. Doc Carroll's got a little shack down the line he uses for a hospital and operatin' room. This hunky got took with pneumonia and was pretty sick for three or four days.

"Mister Spike yonder ambles into my back yard again one night, sits down and howls to the moon just like he'd done before. Mind you, he came up *here*, not down near the hospital. He liked to scare the pants off me."

Rusty broke into a laugh. Rufe turned savagely on him. "Yes, and you too, smart guy. You told me yourself your blood ran cold when you heard that howl."

Rusty nodded. "That's right, Rufe. It does get you."

"Well, what happened?" Dan asked.

Rufe settled back, a look of satisfaction on his face as he dragged a match across the leg of his pants. "Oh, nothin'. Nothin' at all—except next morning the Doc came up and told us the bohunk had died about eleven o'clock the night before."

Dan spoke up. "Was it——?"

"Yes, sir," Martin broke in. "I know just what you're going to say. Was it about the time that Spike was howlin'? It was, within a half-hour of the time the gent passed on. Now, what do you think of that? I tell you the brute ain't human."

The four on the porch were silent. Kirk looked over at Spike, still dozing between the tracks, barely discernible now that the sun had gone down. For the life of him he could not associate anything as uncanny as the predicting of death with the dog. The dog was not human, true, but he was not more than human either. He needed care, love, and

E

attention and gave love and devotion in return. There was nothing uncanny about that.

"Well, what do you think now, Dan?" Martin asked, grinning, enjoying his triumph.

Kirk shook his head. He felt that this was a favourite subject of the station-master's and he did not want to get into a long-winded argument on his first night in Swift River. "It's too deep for me," he said.

Rusty rose to go inside. "Don't let that old guy get you all stirred up, Dan," he warned. "He'd rather argue than eat, and that's sayin' plenty. Quit tryin' to figure out things that're too deep for you, Rufe, and get busy makin' out those waybills for Number Ten. She's due in here first thing in the mornin'. You, too, Jerry, skit! It's way past bedtime."

Jerry stood up, yawned, and retrieved her torch. Dan felt sleepy. It had been a long day. "Hay'll look good to-night. Sweet dreams, everybody. By the way, Martin, are you superstitious?"

"No," came the answer. "Why?"

"Oh, nothing. Only they say death comes in threes, you know. Spike's spotted two already. *Your'e* feeling all right, aren't you, Rufe? Goodnight," he called cheerfully as he started down the path to his cabin, Rusty's laughter ringing in his ears.

Dan heard padded feet trip softly behind him but he did not turn around. After a while he lost the sound, but it did not matter. The moon was out, throwing a sheen of loveliness over the squat empty cabins, the silver river, the tortuous dusty roads leading off into the mystery of the forest, and Dan was lost in his thoughts. He had reached the path to his cabin and had stopped to admire the silhouette of his new home when he felt a soft, moist touch on his arm. He jumped, whirled around to see a shoulder-high pale face staring up at him.

"It's—it's only me." It was Jerry's high voice.

"Phew, you scared me. I guess I'd better not listen to any more of Martin's stories."

The girl stood with him looking at the low, inviting cabin. She kicked a stone that sparkled like a jewel as it tumbled down the path. Finally she blurted out, "I— I'm sorry I blubbered and ran away. You must think I'm an awful sissy. You and Spike were swell. I was so scared I didn't know what to do."

"Forget it. I'd have done the same in your place."

"And thanks for not—for not squealing on me."

"You're wrong there. Rusty and Rufe know."

"Oh." There was dismay in her voice. Dan could almost feel, even if he could not see, her blush. "I fibbed, too."

Dan laughed. "Don't let that worry you. You've got two swell friends in Rusty and Rufe. A little thing like a fib won't bother them. Only I'd tell them as soon as I got around to it if I were you. And don't do anything that'll make them worry about you." Dan held out his hand. "Friends anyhow?" he asked.

The girl's hand was lost in Dan's, the whiteness swallowed up by the tan. She nodded.

"And can I help you with Spike—feed him and wash him and all?"

"Sure thing. We'll tackle him as soon as we've had breakfast."

Jerry released her hand. "I've got to scoot now. Rufe will be looking for me. See you in the morning— Dan."

"So long, kid."

Dan lay for a long time in bed, awake but not restless. He watched a patch of moonlight recede from his chest to his feet. The cabin had a clean smell. He felt very contented, lying there, smelling the sweet smells, listening to the miniature fog-horn of a croaky bullfrog, watching the patch of moonlight. He had found a stopping-off place. He had made a pal, the dog Spike. Friends, a job, perhaps, a job in the woods once more; and strangely enough he found himself looking forward to it. And so thinking he fell into a deep sleep.

It must have been about two o'clock in the morning when Dan was awakened by the wailing cry of a wolf. It started in low register, then mounted higher and higher until it broke into a long chilling howl that had all the terror of a lost soul calling from another world. Again it came—and again. By this time Dan was at the door. It was Spike; squatting on the railroad tracks he poured out his call to the star-studded sky. Down in the station lights suddenly flickered on. Dan could not suppress a grin as he thought of Martin pacing the floor alone. Then Dan returned to his warm bed, pulled the blankets over his head, and went to sleep.

I V

THE WINNING OF SPIKE

THE days following Kirk's settling down at Swift River were periods of instruction and adjustment for both the man and the dog. At first Spike contented himself with a position near Kirk's cabin, coming as far as the door on only one or two occasions. But he constantly trailed along behind Dan as the man went about town helping Rusty with the work of keeping the camp gear in shape. And not once did Spike give any indication of a desire to return to the forest.

A heavy downpour of rain set in and for three days the four inhabitants of Swift River were house bound. Dan had rashly promised to show Jerry how to make her own trout flies from a few chicken feathers, sealing-wax, and thread. They were sitting in Dan's cabin on the second day of the storm, the monotonous patter of the rain in their ears, trying to shape together the wiggling brightly coloured feathers when a sleek dripping head nudged the unlatched door open. It was Spike. He had come to join them after lying for hours just outside the cabin door in all the pouring rain. Jerry ran to get a towel, but Spike would have none of that, nor would he tolerate Dan's attempt to rub him off with a coarse blanket. He shook himself once or twice, dropped down in front of the fireplace, and proceeded to dry himself with his tongue. They let him alone and went about the shack as if the dog did not exist. At first every movement on the part of Jerry or Dan brought instant alertness, but gradually Spike became used to the conditions indoors and snoozed through most of the hours of the storm.

The next night Dan sat beside his table, reading. Outside the rain pelted down in the darkness and the Swift roared and boomed in a swirling flood. Spike lay at his feet, enjoying the gentle stroke of Dan's hand on his head. This delighted the dog and made him feel deliciously drowsy. Whenever the hand stopped its caressing movement across the smooth underside of Spike's jaw or behind his ears, he would nudge the fingers petulantly with his nose until the stroking was resumed.

Kirk held a silky ear for some moments while he

fingered the long welt of a scar. Tracing it, he
found that the tip of the ear itself was ragged, the
notch of an old cut covered by fur. The other ear
was in a somewhat similar condition. Putting
aside his book, Dan dug both hands deep into the
heavy fur along the dog's chest, flanks and hind-
quarters. He found altogether perhaps ten old
scars, ranging from two to ten inches in length,
all completely covered with fur.

"Hmn," he muttered, taking Spike's long muzzle
in his hand and swaying it gently back and forth.
"Had a few battles in your time, haven't you, boy?
Sort of chewed you up a bit, too. Well, I'll bet
you gave as good as you got." He stroked the now
completely healed paw as he studied the dog.

Spike shook his head free from the grip and
thrust his nose into Kirk's hand, a plea for more
petting. Scars to him were things of the past.
Right now the steady caress of Dan's hand was more
important.

The only theory that Dan could formulate to
account for the scars was that some time during the
long winter Spike had joined a pack of wolves in
order to find food or that he had battled the wolves
in order to survive. But Dan was only partly right
in thinking that Spike had at one time completely
reverted to the wild.

It had not been easy for the little cub when he
first sought refuge in the woods. For days the
young dog had gone hungry. He had gnawed
roots and eaten berries, but these were not proper
food for a dog. Small game there had been—

rabbits, squirrels, and birds—but his clumsy, threshing approach frightened them to wing or burrow
out of the reach of his awkward paw. His first
capture had been purely accidental.

Sprawled one day nose down in the soothing
coolness of a forest stream, he sucked greedily at
the water, trying to ease the gnawing pangs of
hunger. A tiny brook trout ventured close to the
shore, stalking a skipper fly that skidded dizzily
across the surface. Little Spike spotted the glisten-
ing fish and slapped a clumsy paw at it. It was a hit.
The fish wiggled wildly beneath the weight of the
paw, and Spike, more alarmed than conscious of
what his success really meant, hastily dragged his
paw inshore, scooping his captive along with a
portion of the river bottom. Then he staggered to
his legs and looked down on the twisting shiny
trout.

For a moment the pup stood, head tilted, barking
at the fish, which in one convulsive leap flipped
upward, striking Spike's inquisitive nose. He had
jumped in alarm but snapped back at the offender.
His sharp little teeth clamped down and in two
gulps he had finished the first solid food he had
tasted in days. It was good, and he spent the rest
of the day roaming the edge of the stream seeking
more trout.

As time went on he had become proficient in this
sort of fishing and he learned to stalk above the trout
silently, standing for long minutes as motionless
as a bronze statue then dipping a paw swiftly into
the water and proudly bringing up his catch.

And so in hunting did he learn patience and the ways of the wild things of the woods. He gradually became expert at slipping noiselessly through the brush, lying in wait for hours as fussy grouse edged closer and closer to his hiding place. Then a flashing paw, and a meal. Larger animals attracted his attention until soon he had become as wary and cunning as any of the wild creatures.

His development was rapid. Perhaps it is not correct to say "development" since he had lost most of the traits that generations of his ancestors had built up by their association with man. However that might be, the fact remains that he grew big, with muscles as tough as leather thongs. He became entirely immune to ordinary discomfitures and learned to endure any sort of weather. To Spike, the idea of Dan's trying to dry him off carried the same significance as smothering would to a human. He could travel for miles without tiring and when, as often happened, he was forced to trail and bring down moose or deer or fight the wolf pack, he was able to acquit himself as though he had been born to the wild. It all seemed to come back to him, all the cunning and patience of remote ancestors, like a lesson learned and forgotten—the trick in circling deer and driving them into deep snow where they would tire easily, the fast leaping in and vicious ripping thrust at throat or belly, then the quick backward jump to safety.

He learned that the wind could be a friend or foe, that in approaching game or eluding a dangerous enemy the wind must be in his face, carrying with it the scent of that which lay ahead. With the wind at his back Spike learned that it was impossible to tell the whereabouts of his quarry while his own presence was unfailingly revealed to the prey he sought.

He learned to take advantage of the snow, knowing that when the drifts piled high the best sleeping place was deep beneath the warm white blanket. There he would bury himself, finding it better by far than some bare windswept space beside a tree or rock. All these things came quickly to Spike and therefore he survived in the wilds.

"Where's Spike, Dan?" Martin called suspiciously, sticking his head through the screen door.

The four had finished breakfast, Dan, Jerry and Rusty were doing the dishes while Martin puttered around on the porch. The morning was bright and warm, the air washed clean by the heavy rain of the night before.

Surprised, Dan looked up from the dishpan. "He's out front, I guess, Rufe. Why?"

"Go see first. I'll bet you a silver dollar he ain't."

Kirk stripped the suds from his dripping arms and stepped around to the front of the station. Spike was nowhere to be seen. Never since that first morning had he failed to take up his position between the rails in front of the boxcar whenever Dan was inside. He had come down for breakfast this morning with Dan and left him to trot out to the rails as soon as he saw that the man was going to stay. Now, he was gone.

"That's strange." Dan's voice had a puzzled tone

as he reported the dog's disappearance to the others.

Martin came inside. He lit his pipe, and his eyes had a light of assurance in them as he leaned against the table and gestured with the pipe. "D'ja feed him yesterday?" he questioned Dan further.

"Sure. He went out and got sopping wet, so I gave him a big batch of corn meal and whitefish."

"Well, he sure must have an appetite," was Martin's reply. "This mornin' he's gone—and another side of my bacon's gone with him."

Rusty spread his dish towel to dry behind the stove and rolled down his sleeves. "I was afraid it was too good to last, Dan," he commented. "It just didn't seem right somehow for that dog to stay put around here. He took quite a shine to you at first. But there's wild blood in him and it'll crop out every so often."

Dan refused to believe it. He did not argue against the dog's disappearance or the loss of the meat: the facts were conclusive. But he would not allow himself to believe that Spike had run wild too long to ever return happily to civilisation, to become a good companion of man. Nor did he believe that the dog would fail to put in an appearance sooner or later.

Jerry did not believe it either. "You're just an old pessimist, Uncle Dave," she said. She always called Rusty "Uncle Dave" just as she called Rufe "Uncle Mart." "I guess he just gets tired of us once in a while. Besides, it's cooler in the woods."

Now Dan was beginning to think that perhaps Rufe and Rusty were right. Spike had not put in an appearance all day, neither at lunch nor supper, and beyond doubt the bacon was missing. That night as Dan prepared for bed in his little cabin there came a bold rasping scratch at his door. Earlier in the evening Jerry had visited him, but she left early so she could get up first thing in the morning and try out her new trout flies. It couldn't be Jerry anyway, or she would have just pushed the door open. Dan rose swiftly from the edge of the bed and threw the door open. In trotted Spike with more assurance than he had ever shown on entering the house. He sniffed Dan quickly, then curled up at the foot of the bed.

Kirk stood, hands on hips, studying him. "Where the devil have you been, Spike?" he demanded severely.

But Spike just cocked his head to one side at the sound of his voice, matched his master's steady stare, then yawned as though despatching the whole thing, and set to work cleaning his pads. Dan dropped down on his hands and knees and examined him from head to foot, searching for evidence that might indicate the hiding place of the bacon. The dog's fur was without a single clue.

Twice in the succeeding ten days Spike disappeared from Swift River. Each time food was missing and each time he was gone for the day to return at night bearing no telltale marks of his jaunt. The last time it had been a partridge which Rusty had shot and hung on his back porch—too high, he thought, for the reach of the marauder. But on the dog's return that night, when the three men examined him for signs of blood and feathers, they found nothing. Spike did not take kindly to this examination. He had no objection to Dan or Jerry, but he growled at the other two whenever they touched him. Martin was especially uneasy when the dog's growls warned him that inspection by strange hands was not relished. Spike seemed to have instilled a real fear in the station-master, who, although he tried to carry the whole thing off as a joke on Dan's continued faith in the dog, was deeply concerned over these strange disappearances, coupled with his belief in Spike's eerie sensing of death. Even though he was proved wrong when nothing untoward followed Spike's third visit to Swift River and the mournful moon call, he was convinced that they "hadn't heard the last of it."

"What's the answer, Dan?" It was Rusty who put the question as they sat discussing Spike's raid.

Dan looked at the dog stretched out on the floor and shrugged his shoulders. "It's got me," he returned slowly. "I've even tried to follow him."

"Get on his trail at all?" Martin asked.

Kirk nodded. "Yes, and that's another funny thing. I picked up his footprints out there in the soft mud near the right-of-way. They led away from the woods over towards that long hill about two miles from here. The trail was hard to find once it led off into the grass, but I managed to pick up a sign here and there and tag along. It made a complete swing around the hill. Then guess what happened?"

"What?" Martin demanded.

"It came right back to where I'd started from. The trail began and ended at exactly the same spot. From there I could find nothing except the one leading back here. What do you make of that?"

Rusty and Martin exchanged glances.

Rufe looked at Spike and scratched his yellow thatch. "He's haunted, I tell ye', Dan. Just plain haunted."

Jerry laughed shrilly in disbelief.

Rusty was silent for a moment. Finally he offered a suggestion. "Let's set watch on the beggar," he said. "Let's keep all the grub inside for a couple of days. You notice he's spaced his runnin' away by two or three days each time. We'll set something out where he can get at it easy. I've got an old pair of field glasses, Dan, and when he leaves we'll hike over to some high spot and keep an eye on him."

"Good idea, Rusty," Dan agreed. "But maybe we'd better be more prepared than that. If he figured we were watching him he'd never move. Suppose the day we leave the food out one of you hoof it down to the water tank. His trail led towards the hill that swings down that way. I'll have to stay around here because if I went out of camp he might take it into his head to follow me. I'll stick around and check on him and the minute I'm sure he's gone, I'll join you."

And so it was agreed. For two days Spike stayed close to Dan's side wherever he went. He had developed a strange little trick of late and seemed to want to display it now more than ever. Heretofore, in trailing along with Dan, he had never shown any disposition to romp or demonstrate affection. But now he would suddenly break into swift charges towards his master, growling and barking, then skid to a halt, bend quickly and grasp Dan's ankle between his jaws. As the growl grew louder, he would shake his head from side to side, but the pressure of his jaws never became too great. Then as quickly as he had charged he would toss his head and romp away, to come suddenly to a walk, striding about stiff-leggedly as if ashamed of his outburst of feeling.

Saturday morning came and through the open door, as they sat at breakfast, Dan could see Spike lying out on the rails, dozing in the sun. "Let's give him the works to-day," he remarked.

The two men nodded. Rufe gulped his coffe. Rising, he went to the cupboard and brought out a slab of bacon. "There she is," he remarked. "Come on, Rusty, we'll coast on down towards the tank. Got those glasses?"

Rusty nodded. Dan called after them, "I'll hang out the bait as soon as you're down the line a bit."

Jerry decided that she would get out her bike and take the more roundabout road. This way, she figured, she would be on the scene first.

As Martin and Rusty came to the track and started walking along the ties, Spike merely raised his head and looked at them. He watched them for a while, and Dan, fearing that he might trot along behind, stepped out on the porch of the shanty on the pretence of shaking a dish towel. He called to the dog, then went inside. Seeing Kirk, Spike was satisfied. His head dropped to his paws and he closed his eyes.

Dan stacked the dishes on the box sink, then took the bacon out to the back of the cabin. Purposely he made considerable noise banging pots and boxes around and a great fuss driving a few nails into the wall. Then he laid the bacon on one of the crates and walked towards his own cabin, calling the dog as he went.

Spike broke into view around the corner of the station, searching for his master. Inside his shack Kirk produced sewing kit and shirt. Seating himself by the door he began to mend. Spike came in and made a circuit of the room, sniffed the familiar furniture, then went outside and stretched out on the ground just beyond Dan's range of vision. For some minutes nothing happened.

After a short while, Dan looked up and saw that their suspicions had been well founded. Spike was down at the station approaching the meat bait as cautiously as if he were stalking a bird. How he had ever left the front of the cabin without being detected Dan could not figure out. But there he was, with every nerve and muscle directed towards the bacon.

Not once did he look towards Dan. His job now was to possess that meat, not only with the least possible noise but also in a manner which would leave no telltale evidence. Slowly, cautiously lifting one foot and setting it in front of the other, he advanced. Then his jaws opened and closed on his loot. Carefully he withdrew until he had cleared the cabin porch. Dan came to his feet and stood watching, fascinated. Once away from the cabin, Spike worked swiftly. He ran across the tracks and down the other side of the railroad embankment. Kirk put his sewing away and started after him, but by the time he had reached the right-of-way the dog was nowhere to be seen. He had disappeared as completely as if he had never existed. Dan hurried on towards the water tank.

His friends waved excitedly as he clambered up the steel ladder leading to the small catwalk encircling the tank, seventy-five feet above the ground.

"Dang'dest thing I ever seen," shouted Martin, looking down at Dan pulling himself up the last rung. Rusty, his eyes glued to the glasses, grinned widely as his gaze slowly swept towards the south.

"He's running in a circle, Dan," Jerry called out excitedly.

"See that hill yonder?" Rufe pointed to a sloping dome about a half a mile away. Kirk nodded. "Well, I'm danged if the dog didn't make one complete circle of that hill and come back where he started from. Lost track of him from time to time when he went to the other side or when he ducked down a ravine but he kept trotting just as steady on his course as any old sailor ever did, luggin' that big chunk of meat all the while, holdin' it high so's it wouldn't drag." Rusty lowered the glasses and handed them to Dan.

"He's out o' sight now," he remarked. "What do

you think he did after makin' that swing around the hill? He came back to where he'd started, turned so he faced the hilltop, crouched, and jumped up the slope a good ten feet. Then he starts on *another* circle. He's behind the rise now. Put the glass on the southeast corner of the slope there, Dan. He'll be comin' into view pretty soon now."

Kirk raised the glasses, adjusting the thumb-screws to bring into focus the spot designated. On the hillside nothing moved. He noticed the grass and the bushes stirring slightly in the wind, the greyish bulk of a boulder, and up almost at the top of the hill a tree stump that had been blasted by lightning. The dead trunk of the tree lay nearby, bare and grey, its shredded fragments rotting at the fracture point.

"There he comes!" It was Jerry who shouted.

Dan turned back to the break of the slope. Sure enough, Spike emerged from behind the hill and was trotting steadily along on a course similar to but at some distance inside, the circuit he had already made. He moved with tireless precision, still, careful to keep the meat high off the ground, thus avoiding all possibility of a scent trail. When he approached a point almost opposite the one where he had begun this series of circles, he slowed down to a walk, then stopped, turned squarely towards the hilltop, and with a mighty spring bounded farther up the hill. At once he was off again, soon to disappear from view.

Three more complete tours he made, each one bringing him closer and closer to the summit.

Jerry and the men watched intently. At last Spike stood about three feet from the blasted stump. With a final leap he was beside it. Carefully he rose on his hind legs and gently dropped the meat into the hollow of the stump. His prize hidden, he lowered himself cautiously, and turning as though on a pivot he leaped away from the hideout, back to the last circular track.

"He's going to back-track on the whole circuit," Martin almost shouted, divining the dog's intentions. Now that they had located Spike's cache they could watch him without glasses. Jerry, however, still used them.

"That's right," she said. "Spike's running on the last circle he made. No wonder Dan couldn't trail him!"

It was true. Spike had already disappeared on the first lap of his return journey. They watched him make a complete swing, jump to the second track at the same place he had crossed before, and then start out again. The observers decided to return to camp. They were chiefly interested now in his arrival home.

About three hours later the dog put in an appearance, not from across the tracks but from the back of the station as if he had just emerged from the woods to the north. He trotted into view, sniffing the ground unconcernedly, paying no attention to the people sitting on the porch. They noticed that his fur was damp and when he lay down in the tracks he immediately began the licking and preening operations all dogs indulge in when wet.

Dan laughed. "So, he's been taking a bath. The pirate! Just to be sure there'd be no sign left on him."

"And did you notice that he came in from the timber?" Rufe offered. "I swear I've never seen such a robber. He takes more pains laying a trail than a surveyor. But it's always the wrong trail as far as we're concerned."

"What do you think now, Dan?" Rusty wanted to know. "What's the best thing to do, now that we've trapped the beggar?"

Dan's smile broadened as he replied. "Face him with his crime, of course, and that ought to be funny. At any rate it's going to be interesting to see the effect it has on Mr. Spike when he finds out we're wise to him. Watch."

Dan rose and walked towards the tracks, not in the direction of the dog but straight to the point where the trail crossed the embankment and down the other side. Spike's head jerked upwards and he came to a sitting position as he watched his master. His nose quivered slightly and his ears pitched forward, all attention. Dan, disregarding him, continued on down the far side of the right-of-way. With a bound the dog was after his master, a whimper trembling in his throat.

"I don't want to miss what happens," Jerry said, and she leaped off the porch and followed the dog. Rusty and his pal hurried up to the rails where they could watch developments, too.

Never did an animal plead and try with all the antics at his command to distract a man more than

Spike did, once he was sure Dan was headed for the cache. With mouth open in a sort of laugh and a funny little whimpering sound vibrating in his throat, he ran alongside his master pressing hard against his legs. Failing to halt Kirk's stride, he crossed and recrossed in front of him as if trying to make him stumble. Then he stopped short squarely in front of the man, reared up on hind legs, slapped big forepaws on Dan's chest, and laughed into his face.

Dan patted him and rumpled the fur along the back of his neck. "What's the matter, old boy?" he said. "Don't like being found out, do you?" Why, I'm just going for a little walk. What's all the fuss about? Come on. You can go along, too."

He lowered the dog to the ground and continued his march up the hill. But Spike was not through yet. He resorted to his pet display of affection, that of grasping Dan's ankle in his mouth. This time the pressure was a little harder than usual and the growl louder. Dan took a slow step, dragging the dog after him, until Spike had to let go. Again the dog secured his hold and again Kirk walked out of it. This kept up until they were within about fifty feet of the stump. Then Spike made one last desperate effort.

He plunged into a nearby thicket, barking and threshing wildly as if he had flushed some important wild game. Looking back at Dan he barked again, a final plea to come and see what he had. Then he raced towards Kirk, leaping and barking, only to lead off again into the bushes, looking back in a last hope that Dan would follow. Kirk stopped and took a few steps in that direction. This was a signal for a fresh outburst. At last it seemed to Spike that he had won, that he had swung his master's attention from the telltale evidence. He bounced around in high happiness over his success, when suddenly Dan changed direction again and marched straight to the stump.

Spike's tail went down and he whimpered sadly. He dropped to his stomach, rested his head upon his paws, and watched Dan with tortured eyes. He knew the game was up.

Rot and decay had hollowed out the stump until it was basketlike in formation. Heaped in a jumbled pile were oddly assorted portions of bacon, birds, chunks of meat, even half-open packages of biscuits. Dan, smiling as he thought of how diversified Spike had been in his choice, scooped the stuff up and walked back down the hill towards the railroad. The dog trotted dejectedly behind, but his master never spoke to him or gave notice that he knew the culprit existed.

Later that night a very penitent dog lay between the rails watching the porch of the little station where Dan and his three friends sat talking. Sorrowfully Spike watched, hoping for some sign of forgiveness. But none was forthcoming as the four ignored him completely. However, his meals during the following weeks tasted strongly of meat flavouring, and he often found juicy chunks of bacon or venison in his mash. This puzzled Spike greatly and also dulled his desire to rob the cabins of food. What sense was there in that if the choice meats he sought were now included in his daily ration?

In the woods, during times of plenty, he had often cached food against periods of scarcity and hunger, a habit he had learned from the wolves. On the few occasions he had entered Swift River, food had been easily accessible, so he had taken it, eaten what he wanted, and hidden the rest. He did not steal the food of the settlement because he wanted to steal. It was because he was hungry and the forest had often been bare of food. In the same way, he did not kill because of any overdeveloped streak of greediness, but to live. Nor did he wolf his food down in slobbering gulps or eat anything he could find because of any gluttonous characteristic, but rather because food was difficult to obtain and often he was starving when he found it. And the sharp digestive acids of the sturdy body he had built up permitted him to eat nearly everything he found or captured.

Yet it is easy to understand why Spike continued his pilfering even after Kirk's arrival, when meals had been regular and food plentiful so that the dread of starvation days no longer remained. To the dog, men were the transient animals. He had crouched in the underbrush and watched Swift River swarm with loggers going into camp. He had seen them again in the spring, finishing up the drive. In his wanderings he had often circled the camps and the cutting areas deep in the forest where for months the jacks were busy getting out timber. Suddenly they would be gone and quiet would settle over the land. How was he to know that this would not happen again, that the man who now saw to it that he was fed regularly would not one day disappear, and that his going would end the period of plenty?

The finding of his food store had two remarkable effects upon the dog's attitude. First if all, it served to break down the last remaining barriers of suspicion towards Dan. Spike became more and more aware of respect towards his master. To him the discovery of the cache was a feat so remarkable that attempts to fathom it only served to make Dan a more remarkable person. Secondly, the possibility of Dan's eventual disappearance seemed to haunt Spike, and from the day of the discovery the fear of losing his master drove the dog to be his constant shadow. He never allowed Kirk out of his sight for a second. He even gave up his post on the tracks, where he always rested when Dan visited Martin or Rusty in the station, and followed his master inside. Here he would lie patiently at Dan's feet, submitting to an occasional mauling from Jerry, but completely ignoring the two older men, much to their disgust. He permitted them to speak to him, but whenever their attentions became familiar he would walk away with a bored aloofness.

Kirk had rigged up a little stove in his cabin and had stocked the cupboard with supplies. Often he ate alone in the shack or had Jerry and the others in as his guests. Almost daily Dan took Spike on hunting trips, where the manner in which the dog stalked game or retrieved it after it was brought down was a source of constant wonder to Kirk; yet game in the field or stores in the cabin, if they belonged to Dan, were never again molested.

However, poor Rufe Martin did not fare so well. It seemed that Spike got real enjoyment out of raiding the gangling station-master's stores, and Rufe promised dire destruction to Spike at every discovery of a loss, much to the amusement of the others, who knew that the old fellow loved to bluster.

Shortly after Dan came to Swift River he had sent to San Francisco for two suitcases, containing all his worldly possessions, which he had left there. Besides some much-needed clothes, he found a gold and platinum wrist-watch that a well-meaning aunt had sent him at the time of his graduation some years before. It was a watch he had never liked, and so he had forgotten about it; but the conductor of the morning freight, who occasionally stopped to have a cup of coffee with Rufe, had a different eye. After much haggling Dan traded the watch to the conductor for a beautiful, well-handled .410 gauge over and under shotgun, which he intended to give Jerry. Both Rufe and Rusty protested, however, that the gift was much too magnificent for such a young kid, and out of deference to them Dan had to content himself with letting Jerry borrow the gun. With Dan as an instructor, Jerry soon became as enthusiastic about hunting as she had formerly been about fishing, and she would drop everything else and come running if Dan suggested a short run up the north road with Spike, for small game abounded in that section of the country. It was on one of these gunning trips that they accidentally unearthed a new cache that Spike had attempted to establish.

Some distance from the village a babbling little stream meandered crazily into the Swift, gurgling and tumbling on its noisy way to the big river. It was a favourite spot of Dan's, and often after their long hikes through the woods he and Jerry and Spike would sit on a log that had been felled across the stream—sit there just resting and soaking up the serenity of the peaceful scene.

On this particular day, after he had been sitting on the log for a half-hour or so, Dan rose to get a drink from the shadowy pool below the log. He drank deeply, then lay there watching the trout dart through the tumbling rapids.

Jerry called his attention to Spike, who had followed him off the log. "Look at Spike, Dan. He seems to have found something." The dog stood at the shore end of the log whining plaintively. He trotted nervously along the bank of the stream, stopping to scoop up mouthfuls of water, then returned to the log's end and whimpered.

Dan watched him for a moment. "What's the matter, boy? Got something you want to show me?" He stood up and walked towards the dog, much to Spike's delight, who now began to rock his body like a seesaw, a manner he had when he was especially pleased. Suddenly he broke into a loud spasm of barking and started down the trail to Swift River. This move brought about his downfall, for well Dan knew that only under the most extreme circumstances did Spike ever bark. Instead of following in the direction Spike indicated, he turned back and walked along the bank. Stooping by the pool again, he studied the silt bottom.

It appeared smooth and undisturbed. Then he noticed a peculiar roll to the contour, and looking closely he made out a reddish form in the swirling weeds. Dan found a stick on the shore. Prodding the odd-appearing lump, he brought to light a full shoulder cut of venison. Three days before Rusty had shot a deer and left the pieces of meat on Rufe's back porch while he ate his dinner. Here, then, was the missing meat.

Kirk fished his find out of the water as Spike lay in the bushes, sadly contemplating this man who seemed to have an unnatural wizardry in unearthing the dog's secrets. He trailed sadly along behind as they made their way home. Once more he was in bad favour.

However, his punishment did not last long this time, and from then on he gave up these attempts to outwit his master.

In fact, his zealousness to impress Dan that he had completely reformed took a new and more embarrassing turn. Everything Spike could steal from Martin he brought directly to Dan's cabin and dropped proudly at his master's feet. His expression seemed to say, "You find everything I hide anyway, so I might as well bring it right here and save us both a lot of trouble. Besides, we'd better keep this stuff, for you never know when grub might run short."

To Dan fell the job of returning the loot to Martin, who would look at the stuff, then glare at Spike and mutter, "I tell you, Dan, there's no sense in us botherin' to go to the warehouse for grub. We'll just hang the keys of the place around that bird's neck and let him go and get what he wants. Then we can follow him and take what's left."

Dan laughed. "May just as well, Rufe. Anyway, Spike and I will invite you over for a meal whenever we make a good haul."

As it had been when Spike, the homeless puppy, was forced to concentrate all his senses and strength upon learning the exacting law of the wild in order to survive, so now, in throwing off the habits of the wild, he focused all his powers on the task of re-adjusting himself to the world of man and to one man in particular. He was too busy doing this to share his attention with anything or anybody else. Dan became his life, and around Dan the whole world revolved as far as Spike was concerned. He never lost the dignity he had displayed from the beginning of their acquaintance, but his adoration for the man grew hourly and was evident in every move he made.

His love of Kirk could be seen in his eyes as he followed his master's slightest move. He would lie for long periods at the far end of the cabin watching the man steadily, the light in his deep brown eyes as gentle and caressing as that in the eyes of a mother observing her child. Indeed, so strong was this gaze, that while he was reading or otherwise busy, Dan would feel its power and turn to study the big dog as if he were drawn by an invisible force. At such time Spike's only means of expressing his happiness was to move swiftly to Dan's side, fall on the floor, and gently take a booted foot between his jaws, clamping down with just the lightest pressure.

Dan would permit this for some minutes, then he would take the long nose between his hands and sway the great head back and forth, softly calling rough terms of affection to his pet, to whom, of course, they were not rough terms at all but sounds that made the heart almost pound its way free from his body in sheer joy.

As Spike developed in the knowledge of the ways of man, so too did his body develop. Rapidly he outgrew the gauntness of a gangling young dog, and his frame took on the rounded grace of the thoroughbred. Power was evident in every step his lean hard legs took, in every ripple of the flank muscles, and in every breath of his broad deep chest. His pelt became as shiny and soft as golden silk, and his movements had the grace of a ballet dancer. He was untiring in the long hunts afield and slept deeply upon his return to the cabin—yet he was awake at the slightest noise.

Satisfied at last that Spike had completely renounced the wild and that he was firmly attached to him, Dan decided that the time had come to start Spike's practical training. The happiness

Dan was experiencing in the dog's companionship would be greatly increased once Spike's native intelligence was moulded into a more responsive understanding.

Dan realised that Spike must, above all, be guided chiefly by kindness and understanding. Radical discipline would serve only to destroy the confidence the dog had exhibited towards himself. Besides, Dan knew that he could never find it in his heart to whip the dog, who already had suffered cruelly from man, nor did he think Spike, with his intelligence, would need the lash of a whip in order to learn to obey. It was Dan's conviction that voice and manner of speaking would play the most important rôle in the scheme he had outlined for Spike's education. Inflections and intonations would do more to carry meaning to the dog than anything else. Commands and word meaning would come later.

So Dan started talking to Spike, carrying on long conversations whenever they were together, addressing the big dog as though he were a child. And as he talked he tried to inject into his voice the mood of the topic he was talking about.

For example, at bedtime Kirk would toss aside his book, yawn noisily, and treat his arms and legs to a mighty stretch. Keeping his voice slow and drawling, he would begin something like this: "Bedtime, boy, bedtime for a couple of lumberjacks"—another prolonged, noisy yawn—"Time to hit the hay"—yawn—"Tough day to-morrow. Dogs have to get their rest, too." Here would begin the undressing operations, starting with boots and shirt. "Go on over and get my bed ready, you faker. What kind of a helper are you, anyway?"

During all this Dan slowly removed his clothes until when he was finally seated on the edge of his cot, Spike would stand before him, head cocked to one side, listening intently, pleading with an occasional whimper to be enlightened on the meaning of all this conversation.

Dan knew, of course, that the dog could not understand a word, but he was sure that a responsive mood was created by the tone of voice as well as by the atmosphere and actions of the definite procedure of preparing for bed. That, to begin with, was all he sought.

Dan varied his methods as well as the cadence of his voice to suit the action he wished to have Spike interpret. When it was time for food, the monologue, fast and exciting, ran something like this: "Time for chow, fellow. Time to put on the nosebag." Here Dan rubbed his stomach and made an elaborate show of getting the material for his own and Spike's meals. "Hungry? What'll you have to-day? Steak or fish? Fried potatoes sure smell good." And so on, and so on. It was all just a little ridiculous, and viewing himself objectively Dan had to laugh, but nevertheless his system seemed to work.

During such a running fire of talk Spike would prance around his master, following him from stove to cupboard, or outside in the case of his own food being set out, with such eagerness that before long he not only recognised Dan's mealtime preparations but came to anticipate them at the same hour every day. Particularly at nightfall, the time when his big meal was prepared, Spike began to move restlessly about Dan, softly whimpering his plea to get started with the meal.

Well pleased with the progress he was making, Dan extended the training to other activities. Getting ready to go outside, whether to visit Rusty or Martin or to hunt, he injected more excitement and animation into the preliminaries. He would make a great show and ceremony of his preparations, clapping his hands and speaking rapidly, holding hat, coat, or gun before the dog so that association of word and action became more firmly impressed by the display of articles of equipment to which Dan referred.

It was not long before Dan merely had to pick up a hat or reach for the gun-rack to bring instant attentiveness on the part of the dog. Spike would run to the door and stand there expectantly, confident that a walk down to Martin's, a tour of the little village, or a day in the woods was on the programme for his master and himself.

The next job was instruction in commands. Once again Dan's theory of association and inflection formed the basis of the dog's training. Well grounded in the fact that Dan's voice varied according to the action of the moment, Spike gave the man full attention whenever he was spoken to.

To start with Dan always spoke his command only when the dog was in the act of doing the thing he was about to be taught. For example, when Spike stood outside the cabin looking through the open door, Dan would invite him in, calling to him in a low voice, pleading, "All right boy, come in. Here, Spike." Then he would hold out his hand or slap it against his thigh. Tone, action, plea, and the fact that Spike had intended entering in the first place, all hooked up with the words "come in" and took meaning in his mind. He would enter to be rewarded with a pat on the head.

When this lesson was learned, a complication was injected. Dan led him outside and left him at the door. When Spike moved to enter, Dan would say sharply, "Stop, Spike—stop there!" The abruptness of the order held him in check, uncertain. Then came the words, "All right boy, come in." The difference was impressive and Spike learned when to move and when to stop.

So Spike progressed. The ordinary commands— "lie down," "come here," "come in," "outside"— were quickly learned, and once clear never forgotten. Indeed, Spike even seemed pleased with his new knowledge; it was another means of serving his master. The work in the field, where he was taught to come to heel, to remain at Dan's side until ordered to advance, to bring small game and drop it in his master's hand or at his feet, took a little more time; but Spike was not gun shy, and once he got it into his head that he was to mouth the game and not bite on it, his education was complete.

The day came at last when the lumberjacks returned to Swift River—noisy, colourful big men, dressed in bright shirts, stagged pants, and heavy boots. Ready for the long winter in the timber, they were as boisterous and cheerful as a group of schoolboys on the eve of a holiday. When this day came, Spike was a great tan dog of beauty, grown out of awkwardness of puppyhood, who looked to Dan Kirk for the order to command his every move.

V

A FIGHT—AND A JOB

OVERNIGHT Swift River had undergone a magic metamorphosis from a sleepy ghost town with four inhabitants to a turbulent, thriving community that vibrated with noise, cheer and bustle. The little town seemed much too small for its teeming inhabitants, but this may have been because, in turn, the husky, broad-shouldered jacks all seemed too huge for the cabins they occupied.

Three or four days before the arrival of the lumberjacks, a freight train loaded with goods of

all sorts pulled into the short siding near the station.
Riding with their goods were the storekeepers, the
merchants of Swift River. By the time the jacks
arrived all these articles—blankets, socks, wind-
breakers, sewing kits, all the paraphernalia a lumberjack needs or thinks he needs—would be unpacked
and displayed in attractive heaps, ready for sale.
Most of the merchants would stay only till the jacks
moved into the brush, to return again in the spring.

Dan struck a bargain with one of them, a little
Scot from Seattle, trading with fresh game for
shotgun shells, small articles of personal wear, and
a green and red wool plaid shirt. The shirt Dan
gave to Jerry "because she had helped him with
Spike." It was of a size for the smallest chore
boy, but it was still too big for Jerry to wear as
a shirt, so she used it as a windbreaker, tucking
the tail into the waist of her jodhpurs. She had
started wearing jodhpurs when ice began to form
along the banks of the Swift, a sign that it was
nearly time for her return to the coast. In turn
she presented Dan with a bone-handled clasp knife
with a single wicked-looking blade. In the same
store her eye had been taken by some bright yellow
woollen scarfs, a half a dozen of which the store-
keeper had stocked as a "flyer." She bought one
each for Rufe and Rusty, much to their outward
disapproval and their inner satisfaction. Even
Spike was not neglected. From the Scot Dan
obtained a broad leather belt with a silver buckle
which he cut down as a collar for the dog. A piece
of brass that he found in the storeroom when he

and Rusty were cleaning it out was hammered thin and riveted to the leather for a nameplate. Dan pricked in the letters with a nail; on top it read, "Spike—Swift River" and underneath, "Dan Kirk, Owner."

Spike seemed to be quite proud of his collar—at least he made no effort to tear it off. He was quite bewildered, however, by the amount of noise and the number of unaccustomed people; the last time he had seen Swift River at the commencement of the logging season he had skulked on the edge of the clearing; and when they walked out he kept closer than ever to Dan's heels.

Both Rusty and Rufe had warned Dan that it would not be politic for him to attempt to see Hart until the latter had had time to get settled. Hart, so Rusty said, was a very poor sleeper who made the habit of getting up an hour earlier and going to bed an hour later than anyone else, and Rusty recommended Dan tackle him early in the morning. So it was not until the third morning after the loggers arrived that Dan found himself walking down the street in the early morning quiet, with Spike at his heels, seeking the camp boss. It was still very early; smoke spiralling lazily to the sky, the occasional clatter of pots and pans, and the fragrant odour of flapjacks, bacon, and freshly boiled coffee were the only signs of life in Swift River.

Dan buttoned his windbreaker tighter against his throat, but his pace slowed despite the cold. He was conscious of a bottomless feeling in the pit of his stomach, and any moment he expected his heart to plummet into this void. Without a thought he had ridden dancing logs down a turbulent river, or dashed in wildly to break up a threatening log jam. Entering a ring with a dangerous opponent, he had been conscious only of the fact that he had a job to do. Now that he was about to face the comparatively mild business of asking a man for a position, he seemed to be really aware of fear for for the first time in his life.

Although he had worked from the time he was fourteen, Dan had never had to undergo the painful and unpleasant experience of asking for a job. But he had often hired men, and now as he slowly walked along the deserted street he tried to recall what had impressed him about the various job-seekers he had taken on.

Thinking back, Dan realised that the men who had impressed him the most were the men who had very clearly showed their independence. Lumberjacks are a pretty independent lot as a rule, but many of them, after spending the first few weeks of their lay-off in riotous drunkenness or a spree of living on a grand scale, would come around begging for work a month before the fall season started. They impressed Dan more with their need for work than their ability to do a job well. The men Dan liked were those who stated their abilities frankly and let him make up his own mind, apparently not caring too much whether he said yes or no. Having a stubborn, independent streak himself, Dan appreciated their attitude. These were the men he hired.

And he knew that this was the only way he could act now. He could do the work; if Hart needed him, well and good; if not, well, that was all right too.

Looking down at Spike trotting contentedly at his side, Dan's heart bounded back to its normal position. The dog's confidence in him gave him more of a thrill than any words of praise. What a difference a month or so had made!

Now the jacks had begun to pour out of their cabins, ready for the work of getting supplies and materials to the camps so that they could start their proper task of getting out the big sticks. Dan had dawdled a long time thinking over his problem. Now he quickened his pace.

But it was something other than his dawdling that prevented him from seeing Hart that morning.

When they were within a few houses of the big two-storey cabin where Hart lived and had his office, Spike suddenly crouched halfway to the ground and refused to go on. His ears flattened, his tail curved down between his legs, and a deep growl rumbled in his chest.

"Heel, Spike!" Dan commanded. This was the first time since the day they had met down by the water tank that Spike had acted this way, and it was the first time since Dan had finished his training that Spike refused to come to heel.

"That's my dog, stranger."

Dan whirled around. Deep in thought, he had not noticed anyone approaching. The owner of the voice was a hulking lumberjack who, despite Dan's six feet one, seemed to tower over him.

Coarse black hair protruded from the open collar
of his red and black wool shirt. His hair was black,
too, and so were his beetling eyebrows. With his
humped, broken nose, thin lips, and black hair Dan
would have taken him for a Turk or an Arab, except
that he was a much bigger man with shoulders like
a cart horse. Dan looked up with a puzzled expression.

"So you say," he replied. "Call him if you
like."

The lumberjack's fists, which were as big as hams,
tightened till his knuckles showed red. He looked
at Dan with a contemptuous expression and then
turned to Spike.

"Here, Spike," he called, bending over and slapping his knees. "Here, boy. C'm'ere."

The man's face flushed a mottled red as Spike,
instead of coming to him, moved off the wooden
sidewalk into the mud road.

"Sure you're right, mister?" Dan asked, bitingly.
"Looks to me as though he doesn't know you.
Now if you don't mind——" Dan started to push by
the big lumberjack and continue down the street.

"Oh, no you don't." The jack stood across the
sidewalk barring Dan's path. "I trapped the brute
and he's mine. Guess you ain't been around loggin'
camps much, mister."

For the first time this seemingly chance encounter
began to make sense, to fit into the picture Dan had
of Swift River and the people who came to it. So
this was the fellow who had trapped Spike and kept
him penned up. Bart—what was his name? Bart

McQuade. From the moment Rufe first spoke of him Dan had taken an intense dislike to a man bearing the name McQuade—mostly because of his cruel treatment of Spike, but perhaps too because Dan was just a little jealous that anyone had attempted to claim Spike before him. Dan looked the big fellow over with more interest. No, he had not liked the man nor his name, and seeing him in the flesh Dan liked him even less.

"I've been around some," Dan replied finally. "Why?"

"Then you'd know a jack's property ain't to be touched."

It was Dan's turn to flush red. Hitherto he had attempted to keep the conversation on a peaceable if not friendly, level. As far as he was concerned, that no longer mattered. The struggle between him and McQuade had been bound to come anyway sooner or later, and now was as good a time as any.

"So the dog's your property?" he asked. If McQuade had been a wiser man he would have taken warning at the calmness of Dan's voice.

"You hit it on the head that time, mister, and I'm claimin' him right now."

Dan coolly looked McQuade over, calculating his strengths and weaknesses as a jack looks over a tree he is about to fell.

"McQuade, you're a rotten liar and a coward. And if you so much as move towards that dog you'll regret it to your dying day."

Dan saw the quick black look of anger flash across McQuade's eyes, preparing him for the rush that was sure to follow. In college boxing circles Kirk had been noted chiefly for his almost diabolical ability to fathom his opponent's intentions, waiting until the last possible second before he twisted away or set himself to deliver the knockout blow when his opponent's mistake had carried him off guard. Keeping his own defensive stance, Dan paid very little attention to the other fellow's feints and manœuverings, but he watched his opponent's eyes like a hawk. Few boxers could prevent this fleeting but definite telegraphing of their intentions. But even if McQuade had known that Kirk had once been heavyweight champion of the Eastern Conference, it is not likely that that would have prevented him from giving this young pup a lesson. He had a reputation as the bully of the camps to uphold, and this lah-de-dah kid with his clipped eastern talk was beginning to get under his skin. Dan was really treading on dangerous ground; McQuade in action was like a giant pneumatic drill gone berserk.

But Dan had been doing some thinking too, planning a campaign. McQuade's jaw was thick and heavy, like a pig of iron. It would do no good to clip him on the jaw in hopes of a quick knockout; besides Dan might break his wrist, and if he was going to work as a lumberjack he needed his hands. No, the solar plexus offered opportunities. At the end of the spring drive McQuade's muscles would be as solid as a pine log, but this was only the beginning of the season, and from lack of exercise and loose living the huge lumberjack was probably flabby.

Dan did not have much time to think. The words "rotten liar" and "coward" rang in McQuade's ears as loudly as the pulsating tocsin of a tremendous "gut hammer." His eyes flashed black, he snorted, and the rush came.

With a little skip, shuffling his feet to gain momentum, McQuade raised his right arm like a sledge hammer and came at Kirk. Coolly Dan stepped aside, his right flicking out straight from the hip to McQuade's stomach while the big lumberjack, looking like a charging bull moose, was just a foot away. A queer puzzled expression passed over McQuade's face. His arms dropped and crossed over the middle of his body; grunting, his mouth open and his eyes popped; and he slowly sank to one knee. But McQuade was not finished yet. It was a clean, well-placed blow, but McQuade had lived in the open for years, and a few month's let-up had not softened his stomach muscles.

Dan moved off and let his hands fall to his sides, narrowly watching the fallen man. Behind him he was conscious of quick breathing no louder than the sigh of a summer wind, and the same time a murmur arose like the hum of bees around their nest. In a few moments the two or three men who had stopped to see the fight had been joined by countless others, most of them hoping to see McQuade get the daylights beaten out of him; and now they formed a ring around Dan and the fallen lumberjack. They looked with admiration on this straight figured young fellow who with one blow had shattered McQuade's immense prestige.

McQuade, meanwhile, remained kneeling on the ground, his hands still clasped around his stomach, his head bowed. Suddenly, catching Dan off his guard, he rose to his feet and charged, striking awkwardly with both fists. This unorthodox punch almost proved to be Dan's undoing; though he parried one of the hammerlike blows, the other caught him in the forehead between the eyes. It brought tears to his eyes, and he was sent back sprawling among the crowd. The presence of the crowd saved Dan then, for if no one had been there McQuade would probably have administered a *coup de pied*—a kick in the head—and that would have been the end of Dan for the time being.

But before he could rise, a snarl sounded somewhere beside him and a whizzing tan form shot out of the crowd and hurled itself at McQuade. It was Spike. For a moment, at the sight and smell of McQuade, the dog had forgotten that now he had a kinder master, and he had abjectly cringed, leaving the man to fight his battles. But the huge lumberjack's attack on his benefactor brought back the full remembrance of the happiest month of his life, and with his lips drawn back in a snarl that would send a chill down the strongest man's spine, Spike threw himself at his master's tormentor.

McQuade struck a glancing blow at the dog that knocked him back on his haunches. In a flash he was at McQuade's throat, and all of the lumberjack's strength could not have saved him had not Dan seized Spike's collar from behind, nearly choking the dog, and led him for someone in the crowd to hold, out of sight of the struggle. This was his fight now, not Spike's.

Before Dan could turn around McQuade, either forgetting or not caring for the rules of the game, moved in and whirled him around with a blow on the shoulder that made all the muscles in his upper arm ache.

Dan quickly recovered and the men stood facing each other, sparring for position. Dan was grinning now, an even grin that got on McQuade's nerves, but his cheeks were tinged with red and there was a strange, fierce light in his eyes.

Careful of his stomach now, McQuade kept his guard in a low position, the massive arms not allowing Dan room to strike home. Realising that his endurance would carry him through to the bitter end, but not wanting to take a chance on one of McQuade's ox-like blows reaching him in some vital spot, Dan decided to change tactics. He aimed at the lumberjack's heart and got in several quick punches at the risk of several smashing returns. Nevertheless he had gained his point. The massive arms were raised as McQuade attempted to protect his chest. Now Dan aimed at the lumberjack's face. McQuade began to lose his temper as the stinging blows brought the blood rushing to his skin, and finally, when one of Dan's jabs cut the skin, he forgot himself entirely. Moving back, twisting his body as he aimed the toe of his heavy boot, he kicked out at Dan's chin. This was a manœuvre commonly practised in the old and dangerous French sport of *savate*, and it is still used occasionally among convicts and backwoodsmen. Dan was surprised, but not enough to prevent him from throwing his head back. The toe of the heavy boot missed his face by inches. Too experienced in the ring not to take advantage of a miss by the other fellow, Dan moved in quickly, and before McQuade could regain his balance he had landed punches thick and fast on McQuade's head and face. One blow in particular, a clip behind the lumberjack's right ear, quickly brought McQuade's fists up to cover his face. This was the chance Dan had been playing for.

Dan hesitated for just a second. It seemed longer to the group of lumberjacks silently watching, who, sensing the drama of the moment, let out audible sighs. Then Dan's right shot out at McQuade's solar plexus with a force that had behind it all of his strength. The thud of the blow gone home was wiped out by the agonised grunt from McQuade that was heard beyond the last row of the crowd. His face twisted, his arms clasped to his sides, McQuade bent forward. Gently Dan's left struck his cheek, raising his head slightly, and the coiled right struck again, landing this time with a crack. McQuade's head jerked back as he fell to his knees. Twisting sideways, he fell on his back, then rolled over on his face. He did not move again. The fight was over.

His breath coming in gasps that seemed to scorch his throat, Dan stood there a moment staring dumbly at his fallen adversary. The onlookers were silent and subdued, too, staring at the prostrate giant. They seemed to find it hard to realise that the man they thought unbeatable had in a few short minutes been knocked into insensibility. Stooping over to recover his cap, Dan noticed that his fingers were puffed and his arms felt as though they were weighted with lead. He picked the cap up and clumsily dropped it again. This action served to release the crowd from the spell which held it; someone laughed, and soon a babble of voices shattered the air as the crowd became articulate once more. As Dan walked towards the men a lane opened for him. Hands reached out and patted him on the back. He could not help overhearing the remarks the men made: " Who is that guy, anyway? . . . . What a right! . . . Looks good to see McQuade on the ground for a change."

Halfway through the crowd a hand reached out, holding his arm. Dan looked up into a smiling face—Rufe, the station-master. "That aboy, Dan!" he said, hitting Dan on the back with his free arm. "It did my soul good to see you lay into that fellow." It was Dan's turn to grin now. "Fine law-enforcin' officer you are," he answered, mimicking Rufe's tone of voice. Rufe laughed and let him go.

On the fringe of the crowd Dan saw Spike. With a muffled bark, Spike broke loose from the person holding him, ran up to Dan, and placing his paws on the man's chest commenced licking his face. His laughing expression seemed to say, "Thanks, pal. I guess you can do all the fighting for us in the future." Dan pounded the sleek sides and ruffed the fur behind the pointed ears before he set his pet back on the ground.

The grizzled clerk shook his head gravely at Dan's request to see Hart. "Sorry, mister, but he went up river 'bout a half-hour ago with some of the boys. May be back this afternoon, may not be here to-morrow. Let's see now, what did you say your name——"

"Never mind. I'll be back again," Dan interrupted. Calling Spike, he walked down by the river to take a roundabout way home, avoiding the crowd still milling on Main Street.

Late that night Dan Kirk sat by the table reading, Spike's head stretched comfortably across his feet, when a sharp rap sounded at the cabin door. A tall thin man wearing tortoiseshell glasses stood outside. Even in the dim light Dan recognised the imposing figure of the camp boss.

"Mind if I come in?" Hart enquired.

Dan stood aside. "Come right ahead. It's the least I can do after living on your bounty."

Hart sat down and Dan pushed his tobacco pouch across the table. When Hart entered, Spike had gone over by the fireplace and stretched out; now he took a few sniffs around the room, extending a questioning nose towards Hart, and seeming satisfied with the results of his enquiry returned to his position by Dan's feet. The crackling of the fire was the only sound in the room as the men packed their pipes and lit up.

Leaning back in the chair, puffing contentedly on

his pipe, Dan narrowly examined the man on whom his fate—or his possibility of getting a job—now depended. Jack Hart had none of the features of his daughter, except perhaps for the peculiar shade of his eyes. His hair was white and combed straight back close to the sides of his head, giving him a gently leonine appearance. Contrasted with his ruddy complexion and his wind-tanned skin, the silvery hair gave him a youthful appearance, so that his face belied his years. Hart's slimness was deceptive. Although not brawny, his muscles were lithe and active, as many a hunky, insecurely relying on superior strength, found out to his sorrow. His every action gave evidence of the assurance that came from long experience in giving orders and having them obeyed.

At last Hart broke the silence. "So this is the wonder dog," he said, pointing at Spike with the stem of his pipe. Spike pricked up his ears and looked quickly up at Hart. The camp boss's voice was gentle, yet he only had to speak in a whisper to have a listener understand every syllable.

Dan smiled. "It seems that I've spent hours just hearing his autobiography. He's done a lot in his short life."

Hart nodded. "Glad to see you've done something with him. Every blasted jack around here's got the idea the dog isn't natural. Why, even Rufe Martin thinks he has some psychic ability. Darn nice dog," he added, reaching over and patting the dog's head. "Even lets me pet him."

"And a month ago he might have taken your hand off."

"Ever work for Northern before?" Hart asked suddenly, giving Spike one last pat.

Dan looked puzzled. "No, why do you ask?"

"Nothing really. Your face looked familiar, and when you started to talk I had the impression I'd known you before."

"Not in this world at least," Dan said, laughing.

Silence settled down on the little group again.

And again it was Hart who shattered the silence. Strangely enough, he seemed embarrassed. Pink overlaid the tan of his skin and he kept his eyes focused on the fireplace, over Dan's left shoulder. "By the way, I want to thank you for what you did for Jerry. I really don't——"

"Forget it," Kirk said abruptly. "Accidents can happen anywhere—even in a girl's finishing school. And if you want to thank anybody, thank Spike here. He's the real hero."

Hart smiled, one of his rare smiles that made him look boyish and mischievous. He seemed happy to get the statement of obligation off his chest, and he reached over to give Spike's fur a vigorous rubbing. Much aggrieved that he had been disturbed, Spike got to his feet with a hurt expression on his face and walked over to the fireplace, where he settled down again with a doggish sigh.

"I'll send him a t-bone steak in the morning. Maybe that'll make up for it," Hart said, knocking his pipe out on the edge of the ashtray. "They tell me you need a job. Know the business?"

For a few moments Dan was silent, thoughtfully watching the smoke rise in the chimney. Hart studied Kirk, a puzzled expression in his wide-set, intelligent eyes. Hart liked the young fellow, liked him for the way he had handled Jerry, for the modest way in which he had dismissed his, Hart's gratitude. He even liked him for beating up McQuade. Of course, the huge fellow was a good lumberjack, but it often got on Hart's nerves the way he bulldozed the other jacks. As long as McQuade's bullying had had no bearing on the business itself, Hart had not interfered, but he was secretly grateful that Dan had taken him down a peg or two. And if he knew anything about character at all, he knew this chap had the stuff in him. But this mysterious business now . . . even Rusty had admitted he did not know Dan's full name.

At last Dan spoke. "Yes, I know the business pretty well. I wasn't going to tell you my right name, but if I do I guess you'll understand why I should know something about logging."

"What's the matter, son?" Hart wanted to know, solicitous at once. "Haven't got yourself in a jam with the police, have you?"

Dan smiled and shook his head. "Not that bad. My name is Kirk."

For a moment Hart looked straight at him. Then he asked, "Jim Kirk's son?"

Dan nodded.

"Knew I'd seen you before. You're the image of your dad. We were kids together. No finer lumberman in the business. I—I'm sorry about what happened. Never did know he was in a bad

way till it was all over.   Why, he was a young man,
too.   He could've called on any of us—me, Mike
Quirk up at pioneer, any of us—we'd all been glad
to back him to the last red cent . . . .   Want to
tell me about it?"

Dan did want to talk.   He had not wished to at
first—he had been afraid to, afraid of his temper.
But as time went on he had been oppressed by a
desire to unburden himself, to get rid of the dangerous thoughts that had been poisoning his mind,
turning him against his kind.   He felt a sense of
security with Hart, who was of the same mould
and stamp that produced his father.   It mattered
little now that he had pledged himself to secure
employment on his own merits and not as the son
of Jim Kirk.

He told of his life with his father and how close
they had been since his mother died when he was
still a youngster.   He told of his days as a youngster
starting work as a chore boy in the camps, lighting
fires, washing dishes, doing all the odd jobs there
were to be done, working from three in the morning
till ten and eleven at night.

Then came forestry school in New York State,
and after that the real education, supervised by his
dad—the job of learning the lumber business.   How
to handle the axe and fell a tree, notching it first,
then cutting through with a crosscut saw and
dropping the big stick right where it was wanted.
Topper, swamping out roads in the heavy brush;
teamster; top-loader.   And in the spring, pike pole
or peavey in hand, skipping across the bobbing,

shifting logs, racing down rivers in the big drive. Time-keeping and timber cruising—in fact every phase of the business had been included in Dan's education. As Kirk talked, Hart realised there was no boasting in his statements—simply facts which had always been a part of his life. Then came the crash.

"We did pretty well, even through the depression. In a small way, of course, but some of the land we held was pretty valuable. Then big interests started to question some of Dad's timber patents." Dan paused, and his eyes, which had been sparkling while he talked of his father, filmed over. "You know in the old days the loggers got the land dirt cheap because the railroads never figured the country would support their building lines through the timber. Well, we were doing all right till the big interests got after Dad to sell out. He refused and they put on the squeeze. We began to have labour trouble. Accidents happened to us and us alone. Then we had a jam and couldn't get our timber out—another accident. Money was tight at the banks and the Great Western Lumber Company, who wanted the property, made it tougher than ever to get. We fought as best we could, borrowed on everything, sacrificed every penny we had in the world to keep the camps going. But in the end they got an injunction and closed down on us. That killed Dad—and it left me broke. But I know it was all a low-down, crooked stunt, and some day I'll get the goods on Great Western and prove they stole our land."

Dan turned and with a decisive gesture knocked his cold pipe out on the fireplace. His face had flushed while he was reciting the downfall of Kirk and Son, and his eyes had an angry fire in them. For a moment Hart was silent, a frown furrowing his brow.

"What did you do when your father died, Dan?"

"Have you ever met J. P. Schwartz?"

"President of Great Western? No, but I've heard of him. I guess everybody in the lumber business has."

"Well, I have," Dan continued, stabbing the table now with his clasp-knife. "It was only for a few minutes. He came to Seattle to see Dad about selling out. But the figure he offered! Anyway, he has narrow slits of eyes like a cat—they weren't little and round like a pig's, oh, no—he looked as though any minute he was going to pounce. Well, I couldn't get those eyes out of my mind. I thought I'd go crazy at first trying to think of some way to revenge Dad and myself on those cat's eyes. But what can you do when the intended victim is two thousand miles away and he has scads of dough and the law on his side and you're lucky to have one red cent to rub against another?" Despite his light words, Dan's tone was bitter now, and Hart could sense the venom behind Kirk's thoughts. "I guess it must have made me just a little crazy. I was broke—really broke. I didn't want to ask anyone around our diggings for a job. Finally I hit the road. I may be imagining it, but for a time I was sure Schwartz had me tailed. Then I found myself on a fast freight headed towards Chicago—where Schwartz has his office. They unloaded me, Spike found me, and I don't know, the whole picture changed. Here was Rusty and Rufe and Jerry—and the dog—and Swift River. I began to feel a little more like my old self, and so here I stayed."

As Dan reached the end of the story, his voice became quiet again and the angry look left his eyes. Hart reached over and helped himself to Dan's pouch. The room was beginning to feel chilly, so Dan got up and piled more logs on the fire.

"You know," Hart began reflectively, "your story interests me—in a different way than you think. Schwartz—in the form of Great Western—offered to buy us out last season. The price was ridiculously low, too. We're pretty backward here—don't use many up-to-date methods. Started during the depression, and most of us either owned our own companies or had been big shots in one way or another. Anyway, we do our best to cut down costs, but our holdings are pretty valuable, and we're rather proud of what we've done. So we haven't any intentions of selling out. So far, though, we haven't had any trouble."

"I hope for your sake I'm wrong," Dan replied. "But my instinct says, where J. P. Schwartz is concerned, watch out!"

"It certainly won't hurt to be a little extra vigilant. And I'm grateful to you for tipping us off."

Dan nodded his head and turned and thoughtfully watched Spike where he lay dozing in front of the fire. At last he turned and looked squarely at Hart. "Well, that's my story, Mr. Hart. Do I go to work?"

Hart got up and reached for the light windbreaker he had thrown over the back of the chair. He stuffed tobacco into his pipe, lighted it, then walked to the door. He turned back and smiled at Kirk.

"To tell you the truth, Dan, I came over here thinking that you were just another obligation Jerry had dumped on my lap. I thought I'd be generous and give you a job swamping roads." He laughed. "You sure do, Dan. You'll go in as my time-keeper to begin with. We'll move up to the camps in about a week. Good-night."

Spike was rudely awakened and his sleek sides were pounded by a grinning, very happy master who nearly crushed his ribs as he hugged the dog's furry neck.

Spike thought it all just a little ridiculous, and he merely licked Dan's hand as though to quiet his outburst of happiness.

who nearly crushed his ribs as he hugged the dog's
furry neck.

Spike thought it all just a little ridiculous, and
he meekly licked Dan's hand as though to quiet his
outburst of

VI

CRUISING THE BIG STICKS

DAN KIRK puckered up his lips in an attempt to
whistle as he slogged along the trail in snowshoes,
but no sound came forth; it was too cold. He was
happy nevertheless, even if he could not give vent
to his joy in music. On up ahead ran Spike, serving
to break trail, although mostly he just romped like
a schoolboy getting a taste of the first winter snow.

In a steady, plodding gait that ate up the miles,
Dan headed along the familiar trail towards the
warm cabin deep in the woods. Knowing the land-

marks, the trees, bushes, and outcroppings of stone as another person might know the houses on his street, Dan paid little attention to the country around him and spent most of his travelling time thinking. Recalling now the events of the last few months, he was well pleased with himself.

He remembered with a grin how Jerry, very untomboyish at the last, tried hard not to cry as she bade her father and her four friends (counting Spike) good-bye till the following year.

Then came the long trek up to the camps. Northern Lumber maintained four camps staggered on either side of the Swift, the farthest north being about seventy-five miles from the town of Swift River. Dan had been stationed at Camp Two, on the left bank of the river.

Hart had been quite correct in stating that Dan would find nothing new and modern about Northern's camps. Kirk and Son had prided themselves on their sanitary, up-to-date camps, communities where a man could raise a family, with schools, stores, and a hospital. Here in Camp Two the bunkhouses and cook shanty reminded Kirk of some of the camps he had seen as a boy; but even though they were of the same order as the old-time buildings, they were cleaner, warmer, and better built.

The temper of the men was as different from that of the loggers as were the buildings. In the old days the loggers spent their short leisure hour before bed in trading tall stories, drinking, or indulging in a drag-'em-out form of fighting that was as wasteful in good labour as it was cruel. Now the men spent their leisure reading papers, magazines, or books, or listening to the radio. The men were still tough, make no mistake about that; they had to be, toiling away at the backbreaking work of felling the trees and getting the logs down to the bank of the Swift, working outdoors in all kinds of weather and in temperatures that reached fifty below zero. But they were cleaner, better-living men, and many of them had an ambition to become something higher than a mere foreman. In Dan's bunk there were even three or four college graduates, one of them an ex-full-back, another working as a logger to earn money to continue his post-graduate work.

Unfortunately, McQuade was also posted at Camp Two, although Hart casually mentioned that he intended to send him up to Three later in the season. Once McQuade started to take issue with Dan about some minor detail, but thought better of it and walked away. He made no attempt to reciprocate Dan's ordinary, friendly advances. Seeing Spike trotting around everywhere with Dan seemed to be a constant thorn puncturing the lumberjack's self-esteem. Everyone, including Hart, remarked on the new and different McQuade; they found the change restful even if McQuade was as sullen now as he had formerly been boisterous.

Entering Hart's cabin one evening about two weeks after they had moved up to the camps, Dan found the camp boss at a wide table, nearly submerged in charts.

"Hello, Dan!" he called out without raising his eyes from the maps. "Pull up a chair. I want to talk to you."

Kirk sat beside Hart and leisurely began to fill his pipe, Hart leaned back, accepted the proferred pouch, and while he blew voluminous clouds of blue smoke up to the ceiling, cast a questioning eye on his protégé, as he had started to call Dan.

"How do you like it here by now?" Hart suddenly asked.

"Begins to feel like home," Dan replied, smiling. "I even like the smells."

"Let's hope you're not too comfortable. I've got another job for you." Before Dan could question him, Hart leaned over the chart and pointed a roughened finger on a spot about the shape of an apple. "Here's Camp Two, where we now are, and here's the Swift. Up north a bit is Camp Three on the north bank of where the Cranmer joins the Swift. To the north and south of the Cranmer is the property I want you to look at. It's government stuff and we might start cutting there next year."

Dan's eyes lighted up. Of all the innumerable tasks connected with logging, he liked cruising timber the best. It was an art he had learned well from his father, and he had often walked along a "forty" of mixed pine and spruce, paced off its four sides, then cut diagonally through from corner to corner, and come out with an uncannily accurate estimate of the number of board feet in the stand.

"Swell," was his answer. "When do I start?"

"Hold your horses. There's one thing."

"Yes?" Dan questioned.

"I have heard—now this is only a rumour, mind you—I've heard that Great Western's very much interested in the same property."

Dan whistled.

"From what you tell me," Hart went on, "anything J. P. Schwartz is interested in he eventually gets. Maybe so, maybe not. But forewarned is forearmed, so watch your step. Now let's go over these charts."

For an hour or so the two heads bent over the maps like conspirators. Ranger cabins had been dotted all throughout the district; these were stocked with staple provisions, and Dan could hole in any of them should the weather become too rough. For two summers surveyors had been in the district, running section lines two yards wide, and cleaning out around section and quarter-section posts. Dan should have no trouble finding references for his notes. If Dan felt that he needed anything, he could check into Camp Three or, if he was in the south district, to Camp Two, since that was the nearer. At any rate he was to report his progress every so often,

Until late that night Dan sat up in his bunk hugging his knees, too excited to sleep. He was to be off on his own again, on a job he loved! And with him would be Spike. He had often worried about the dog's running loose around camp. He hated to keep him shut up, but it was not safe to let him wander as he liked, constantly in danger from falling trees, fast-moving sledges, and shifting piles of logs.   Out in the woods he could do as he pleased.

Then there was the possibility, hinted at by Hart, of trouble with Great Western. Although his settling at Swift River signalled the end of his blazing, unreasonable desire for revenge, he still had many old scores to settle. If he played his cards right there was a chance he could unearth enough evidence to restore his father's reputation— and there was always the possibility that he could recover the stolen property of Kirk and Son! Besides, he was still young enough to appreciate a good fight, no matter what the cause, provided it was good.

At the end of the week Dan and Spike crossed the Swift and were soon lost among the towering forest giants.   Hart stood on the opposite bank and watched till the tiny figures were out of sight, then he slowly turned back to his cabin. Life in Camp Two would lose some of its sparkle now, with Dan and the dog away. The camp boss had to smile at his melancholy. "Must be getting old," he muttered, then straightened his back and quickened his pace.

Dan Kirk was the kind of man who asked for little and whose needs were simple. He had never been held in any one place through love of possessions nor was he deterred from going anywhere he liked for the fear of being without the comforts of city life. He found no great difficulty in transporting all his most cherished goods in one small suitcase. So it was now in the woods. Given a little tea, some salt and bacon, he could travel through the uncharted timberlands for days, living off the land like an Indian, and like an Indian, too, feasting when there was plenty and doing without when game was scarce. With Spike he revelled in the job of cruising among the giant trees, sleeping where night found them, circling back after days in the field to one of the ranger shacks for rest and repair of gear.

To Spike the life was a never-ending delight. For weeks on end they would travel. At intervals Dan would stop and consult his charts, locate the surveyor's posts, then apply himself to the job of estimating the number of feet in each timber stand of every section. While his master was thus engaged the dog would plough through the snow in the ecstasy of his freedom or would bound along the trail of a hapless snowshoe rabbit who had used the poor judgment of appearing while Spike was in the neighbourhood. He was ruthless in his hunting, killing with all the ferocity of a wolf, a throwback of the days of necessity when he had to hunt his food.

Being holed up in the cabins by storms were periods of contented loafing for both man and dog. In the evening, as Dan sat making out reports or reading, Spike would lie at his feet and look up at his master with a soft light in his eyes, an occasional whimper of joy sounding in his throat. When Dan looked up the big dog would express his pleasure by suddenly grasping Dan's hand or foot and holding tightly while his big tail thumped against the floor.

Kirk would respond to this attention by talking aloud for long minutes to the dog or by holding his fine head between his hands and muttering roughly as fingers caressed the smooth fur along Spike's jaws.

But Spike's return to the wild where he had roamed alone for a year or more seemed to reawaken the habits that Kirk thought the dog had forgotten. The strain of the wild still throbbed in his blood. He could not easily forget the hunts he had had, the long struggle for survival; the call of the great forests rang in his ears, tempting him from the easy life he now lived to the harder, but more exciting life that the wild animals knew. Had it not been for Dan he would have responded at once to this primitive urge that came again when he returned to the forest. No cabin or fireside could have held him. Kirk alone was the reason for the dog's not ranging the wild at will.

He sat by Dan's fire, a great, broad-chested dog of golden beauty, dreaming constantly of shadowy outlines which seemed to well up before him from the bottomless depths of time.

So strong and moving were these shadows which came to Spike as he lay drowsing that he could almost smell the sweet odour of hot blood and feel the dry, parched feeling in his throat as he travelled in spirit with the wild ancestors he had begun to emulate before the coming of Kirk. Over and over again he hunted with them, running endless miles on the trail of meat, lying half starved for a day as he stalked a wary partridge, or splashing hot and thirsty in the coolness of a deep, green forest stream.

And as these dreams passed before Spike, physical reactions to them took place. Realising what was happening, Dan watched the dog to see what he would do. Spike lay with his head on his paws, to all appearances sound asleep. Suddenly his ears twitched, then cocked alertly as he listened. His head came up and he looked straight at the wall as if his gaze had passed on through the logs, across the miles of snow and timber. Slowly he rose to his feet, and without a single look at the man padded swiftly to the door, reared up, knocked the latch loose, then dropped down and disappeared into the night. Dan let him go, knowing that when the spell had passed he would return more docile than ever.

And return he did always, but not until the urge had spent itself. Perhaps he would be gone for hours, racing through the forest till he had reached a clearing where a slight rise in the ground permitted a wide panoramic view of the silent country. Or perhaps he would startle a rabbit or grouse. If so, then he would crawl as silently as a shadow beneath some thick covering of bush and lie there for hours until the bird had settled down once more—and disclosed his sleeping hideout. Then Spike pounced and ripped and chewed. After that he would lie listening to the sounds of the woods, the crackling of stumps as the frost crept in and split them open, the soft thump of snow as it slid from over-loaded branches, the far-off wail of a wolf, or the hoot of a owl.

Suddenly Spike would remember his master, then he was up like a flash streaking towards the cabin.

He would paw boisterously at the door, demanding entrance, and once inside he would leap and romp about as if trying to distract attention from his disappearance.

Knowing the dog's background, Dan could understand some of the struggle taking place within the animal. For that reason he wisely allowed Spike's emotions to rule him and banked on the dog's affection for him to overcome these wild urges.

But Dan was constantly haunted by the fear that some day the dog would not return. He had become so attached to Spike that the idea of being without him was unthinkable. The lonely woods would be bleak indeed if he had not Spike to share his companionship. The dog had become part of his life, an integral factor in the scheme of things as far as they concerned Dan. Secretly he longed for the gradual disappearance of these long forays into the woods, and the day when he could assert his own will and love over the dog.

And one night the thing that he had long dreaded finally did happen. Spike failed to return.

Spike had stirred uneasily after supper, and at last, roused from a deep sleep at Dan's feet, he rose and trotted outside.

Watching him go, Dan called out, "All right, old globe-trotter. Don't be gone all night." Then he had gone back to his work of plotting timber estimates on the chart. At eleven o'clock Dan undressed and went to bed. The dog had not returned.

Far away on the snowy slope of a hillside Spike lay listening to the night sounds of the wild. He had

had his chase and run, and now he lay panting happily, his mouth open, red tongue dripping. Suddenly he sprang erect, the hair along his spine standing stiff, his muscles quivering. From afar came a call—a wailing, hideous, pleading call. Spike had heard it many times before and he knew that no dog ever uttered such a sound. In a flash he was off, streaking along the shadowy aisles of the forest like a phantom. Again the call came—and Spike, his nose questing the wind, changed his course. As he drew near the source of the sound, he slackened his pace and brought more caution to bear in his approach. He moved closer to the trees and kept to the shadows ; and always he travelled with the wind in his face.

He came to the edge of a clearing and stopped. Black objects sprawled upon the snow in the open space, and a chopping, sucking sound came to Spike as the wolves gnawed the snow from their pads. One sat away from the rest, his nose raised to the sky. From his throat came the age-old call, half sob, half wail, a defiance against the sadness of life itself. When it was done, the wolf's head dropped, and all was still except for the wind moaning softly in the treetops and the sucking sounds as ice was freed from between sharp claws. Spike moved closer, every nerve tense, his body gathered in a half-crouch, his feet moving with infinite care—every motion typical of the meeting of wild things in the forest. The three wolves lying down suddenly noted Spike's presence. With whirling leaps they were up and away. Spike did not follow, for the fourth—the one whose howls had attracted the dog—had come to his feet and was also crouching as he snarled and clipped his teeth together in a rapid series of snaps.

Spike circled. He was larger and heavier than the wolf, but in no way did he overmatch him in cunning and ferocity. Suddenly the wolf sprang at the dog, sprang so quickly that he missed the throat hold and smashed against Spike's shoulder. Over the two of them went, threshing wildly in the snow. The wolf gained his feet first and slashed viciously at Spike's shoulder, then leaped clear. Before the dog could recover, the wolf had leaped in twice more; but each time Spike drew back, to hear the other's teeth snap dangerously as they missed their hold.

Spike knew that this was to be a finish. His urge to return to the wild had brought him face to face with the inevitable law of the wild—kill or be killed. All resemblance he may have had to a civilised dog rolled away from him as he stood there, teeth bared, awaiting the wolf's rush—a killer of the wild.

In the white arena of the clearing everything was still. Even the wind seemed to have died down as if pausing to watch this battle to the death. Only the breathing of the two could be heard, and their breath rose in the still air like frosty veils. Their eyes gleamed yellow in the half-light as they slowly circled, treading a path in the snow, each watching the other for some misstep that would offer an opening.

The wolf's rage was bitter but not blind. When he rushed, it was because he fancied he saw an opportunity for the death grip. Again and again he slashed at Spike, bleeding now from a score of cuts. The dog, however, bided his time. Only once did he drive at his adversary, and then he succeeded in chewing off nearly all the wolf's ear. Whenever the wolf's teeth touched the soft, tender flesh of the dog, he was repulsed by Spike's teeth. Time and time again Spike felt the other clawing for the throat hold, that soft spot beneath the jaws where warm blood runs close to the surface, but each time he had been able to throw off the threat by a counter-attack.

At last Spike took the offensive and began to rush. Using his size and weight, he would feign a dive for the throat, then turn his head and slam with all his strength against the wolf's side. Every time he tried the rush his shoulder was slashed anew, but there was a plan in Spike's mind and he suffered the teeth in his shoulder to carry the plan through.

The snow was dyed red with blood—mostly Spike's. A hard path was worn in the snow. Patiently Spike continued his seemingly futile attack. Rush, slam, then a click of teeth as they sank into his shoulders, then the spring back, the pace around and around for position, and the same thing all over again.

Finally the chance he played for came. Gathering himself for the smash at the wolf's side, a manœuvre that had confused the animal and for which he had no defence, Spike shifted suddenly, and as the other drew his head high and braced himself for the impact, Spike dived fair and true for the throat. Like a steel trap his jaws clicked shut around the soft flesh, and with a mighty heave he tossed the other

over on his back and held on. It was all over. Spike
let go at last, sniffed the dead animal once or twice,
then sat down to lick his wounds.

For a long time Spike lay there ministering to
himself. Occasionally he looked over at the stiffening body of the wolf and once he hobbled to it on
his stiff and sore legs, growling at the inert thing.
Then he flopped to the snow again and nursed himself till dawn.

At last Spike rose and limped away into the woods.
He came to a spring in the hillside, lightly covered
with glasslike ice. He crushed through with his paw
and drank. Then he found a drift and curled up to
sleep. It was late afternoon and dark again when he
awoke. His muscles were sore and tired, but no
fever throbbed in his wounds. Gaining his feet, he
trotted off towards the cabin, true to his course as a
mariner.

Dan was sitting down to a lonely supper when
Spike crashed against the door, demanding entrance.
Once inside, he jumped up at Dan and started licking
his face. Dan started to pound the dog's sides till he
noticed the ugly wounds, then he contented himself
with crushing Spike's ears.

"So, you've come back again, you old pirate, you
dirty stay-out-all-night," Dan muttered, swaying the
big head in his hands. "I thought you'd left me for
good. Don't ever try to pull a trick like that again,
mister, or you won't get in when you come home."

Spike slapped a big paw on Dan's wrist and
growled. He looked up into Dan's eyes as if to say,
"Go on, that's old stuff. I don't scare that easy."

Kirk tried to patch up the cuts on Spike's shoulders and flanks, but the dog would have none of his nursing. He treated them himself, and in a few days there was no evidence of his fight with the wolf except a new crop of freshly healed scars.

After his return that evening Spike did not venture forth again after dark. He satisfied himself with the exercise he got on his excursions with Kirk and was content to stay by the fireside. When Dan did let him out to run, he would trot around the cabin two or three times, sniff daintily at the air in the distance and then demand to be let in. Dan laughed. "You're gettin' to be an old grandaddy," he said on one of his periodic tussles with the dog. "Soon I'll have to get you a pair of specs and a pipe."

As the weeks went by, and Dan had checked a good bit of the property in the district, he realised the immense value of the land. The timber grew thick and tall, and there was very little undercutting of brush to be done. The Cranmer River meandered through the stands in such a way as to make an easy river haul from almost any location in the district.

One afternoon Dan stood on a little promontory overlooking a sea of green. "I'll bet there's enough spruce and white pine here for ten years' cutting," he said, speaking out loud. "No wonder Schwartz wants it. And he'll probably sell his soul to get Hart and his gang out of here. Well," Dan continued fatalistically, "it just means more stealing now that we are here. If Schwartz wants this stuff, it's a hundred to one he'll get it unless some outfit's got a cast iron deed to it."

So far, though—and this Dan admitted regret-fully—he had come across nothing to arouse his suspicions. Outside of the marks and the trails left by the surveyors and the occasional tiny range cabins, there was not another evidence of man's touch in the whole property. The only people he had seen in the months he had been out here were the jacks from the various camps where he occasionally appeared, staying overnight, for supplies. He had a feeling—an illogical feeling, true, but when a person lives alone for any length of time he relies more on his hunches and instincts—he had a feeling that there was not another human being within a radius of a hundred miles.

The next morning broke clear and cold. It was the last week in January. Dan stacked the breakfast dishes and then turned to Spike. "Put on your over-shoes this morning, old boy. We're going to hike into Camp Three. Let's see, we're all out of salt for one thing; for another, I could use some coffee for a change. And then I guess old man Hart'll be glad to see us, eh?"

Camp Three was a day's hike from where Dan had been working for over a month. He had made the trip once before over an old trail beaten down by the survey party when they ran their lines into the timber.

Dan did not realise how bitter cold it was till they mounted the rise south of the cabin. The sun was just coming up. Dan carried only a couple of sand-wiches in a side pocket. He could make camp by six, and there would be a warm fire and plenty of hearty food. There was no sense of burdening himself with a pack going in. He would have a heavy enough load coming back.

Spike raced along ahead, throwing up a cloud of snow as he floundered through the drifts. Every once in a while he hid behind some snow-covered clump of brush, and as Dan approached, sprang out at him with mock ferocity, only to dash away whenever the man attempted to grapple with him. And so the morning passed agreeably.

At noon Kirk stopped and, brushing off the top of a tree trunk, munched his cold meat and bread, tossing bits of it to the patient Spike, who sat looking longingly at the food. Dan sat there for fifteen minutes or so, resting, and then they pushed on.

They came to a spot where the trail dipped down to cross the Cranmer, which was about half a mile wide at that point and frozen solid two feet thick. Despite this sheet of ice, the surface of the river was pitted with pockets covered by thinner, glassy ice where small pools had formed by overflowing hillside streams that flooded the surface of the river.

Kirk had spent enough time in the woods to know about these pockets and their dangers. Certainly he knew that they were to be avoided. But he was slogging along deep in thought, wondering about Schwartz and Great Western and whether or not Hart had had any labour trouble, a sure indication of further trouble to come, when suddenly, without warning, he crashed right through one of the pockets into water well over his knees. As he clambered to solid footing he cursed his own stupidity as well as

J. P. Schwartz and the Great Western Lumber Company. Spike, who had been on up ahead, rushed back, and stood silently watching his master strip the fast freezing scales from his socks. Then he trotted along as Dan made for a small clump of niggerheads along the shore.

"Darn fool me," Kirk muttered. "Of all the greenhorn tricks! I've got to get a fire going and dry these socks mucho pronto or I'll end up with a pair of nicely frozen feet. Of all the boneheaded stunts!"

Reaching in the pocket of his mackinaw, Dan muttered a silent oath. Slowly he withdrew his hand and he felt a stab of uncertainty shoot over his breast. His match safe was not there. He remembered now—he had been wearing a lighter buckskin windbreaker in his cruising work and had forgotten to shift the match case over that morning. He had been careless because the walk to Camp Three seemed to be just a stroll. Well, if he could not make a fire it was going to turn out to be much more than a stroll. Hurriedly he searched every pocket. One lone match was his reward. He found it nearly hidden against the seam and fuzz of an inside pocket. Putting the wooden end of the match between his teeth, he gathered some dead twigs and green brush. The brush he used to sweep away a place in the snow, then laid it down to form a base for the fire. Carefully he arranged his twigs, and when all was ready applied the match. For just a moment the flames flickered weakly; then they caught, and a small cheery blaze weaved through the dry stuff.

Rubbing his numbed hands, Dan grinned happily

as he saw the fire mount. Squatting down, he began to unlace his moccasins, which were now completely covered with ice. Spike flopped down beside him and lifted a paw to chew out the ice clinging to his pad. The paw was snow-covered, and as neatly as a tossed ball a handful of snow arched through the air from the dog's foot and landed squarely in the centre of the fire. There was a hissing spurt, then the flames sizzled coldly to extinction. Spike, his head tilted inquisitively at the destruction he had wrought, looked quickly at Dan, then he went on chewing his pads.

For a moment Dan was too startled to act. Then he seized a smouldering twig and, kneeling, attempted to blow it back to life. It was no use, so quickly had the moisture sunk in. His jaw tightened. What had started out as a stupid, thoughtless accident of small proportions now took on a serious aspect. The cold was becoming more intense. His nose and cheeks needed constant rubbing to keep the blood circulating. Now his wet feet were becoming numb and all hope of drying his footgear was gone. Well he knew the fallacy of keeping his feet warm by walking or running. It simply does not happen. The pound of the foot against the ground in its chilled condition drives all circulation upward. There is only one answer-fire. Since he had none, the only alternative for Dan was to start walking and hope for the best. He figured he was about fifteen miles from camp. If he walked far enough he might, by luck, meet an extended cutting party. That was the most he could hope for.

"Come on, old boy," he called quietly to Spike. "We're shoving off." The dog looked up, wondering at this sudden change of plan. But as Dan hurried along the trail, Spike rose and trotted after him.

Kirk set himself to a steady pace, yet he could feel the numbness creeping up around his ankles. He knew it would do no good to trot. In fact, it would be just the thing not to do. He would only expend his strength and not combat the frost in his feet in the slightest. He set his teeth and grimly plugged along.

The sun swung down near the treetops and a fresh chill came with the shadows. There was no wind, and the increasing cold cracked in the dead tree trunks and banged loudly from the river. Dan kept rubbing his face with his mittened hand, but no matter how much he rubbed his cheeks they tingled quickly as soon as they were left unprotected.

After an hour, Dan found that he could hardly walk. His feet seemed detached from his body and he caught himself stumbling. Once he nearly fell on Spike, who leaped out of the way in time and looked up at the man with startled surprise. The numbness had reached Dan's knees now, and he floundered along the trail ankle-deep in snow. Each time he fell —and he fell often—he managed to regain his feet. His feet felt as though they were asleep and it became increasingly difficult for him to direct their movements.

He sat down at last and tried to pull off his wet gear. So solid were the moccasins frozen that he had to remove his mitts to loosen the laces. Doing this

his hands became numb. Even though he hastily slipped them back into his gloves and beat them furiously against his sides, the blood refused to return to his fingertips.

Spike sat on his haunches watching the man. Dan beat his feet with his clenched fists, but it was no good. It was like striking lumps of clay with lumps of clay. He felt himself growing drowsy, and once while he was trying to claw his mitts off to put his hands against his stomach beneath his shirt, he felt an almost uncontrollable desire to sleep. He caught himself nodding, and his head jerked upright. Despite his efforts at resistance, he felt a soft murmuring sound in his ears like the ripple of water from far off.

He dreamed that his wrist was fastened to an iron chain and that the chain was connected to a winch and that a donkey engine connected with the winch was slowly drawing him by the wrist through ice-cold, freezing waters. He awoke with a start, wide awake for the minute, fully aware of the danger of falling asleep. Spike had hold of his wrist and was tugging at his master's arm. Dan's hands felt warmer where Spike had leaned against them. Staggering, Dan stood on his feet and slowly pulled his mitts halfway on.

He couldn't stop now, he couldn't! He was still ten miles or so from camp. No one would be out this way, no one was expecting him, not even Hart. The thought of Hart sent new strength through his nerves. Saying to himself that Hart needed him, that Hart would have a hard time finding as good a cruiser as Dan, that he was the only one who knew the machinations of the Schwartz machine, Dan summoned the will to move a few hundred yards. He stumbled, tripped, and fell. But each time he managed to hunch himself up again. Finally his legs would move no more. The magic strength of Hart's name had lost its potency. Dan crawled a few feet till he reached a tree stump and lay against it.

Now hate was the only thing that could keep him alive. He thought of Schwartz, of the man's black, thin-lipped, cat-eyed features. He thought of his father and how fine a man he had been. He pictured the camps of Kirk and Son. And the fine picture of the past contrasted with the bleak picture of the present sent his heart beating and the blood flowing through his veins. But it could not keep him warm, nor could it keep him from sleeping. Spike moved closer to Dan, putting his body against Dan's. Dan could feel the dog's warmth creep up to him, but it was a deceptive warmth. In time it would pass, and he would be no more. With his last strength, Dan pushed the dog away from him and pointed down the trail, mumbling something that was scarcely audible. Then his chin fell on his breast and he slept. And as he slept the moisture formed near the end of his nose, quickly freezing till Dan looked as though he had forgotten to shave.

Spike looked at the man for some time. Slowly he came back and approached Dan, his nose out-stretched, the hair along his back stiffening. A rumbling growl sounded deep in his throat, a sound of complete bafflement. He made a circle around the man and the stump, sniffing all the while.

Then he sat down. The shadows had lengthened and it was quiet and dark on the trail. Spike whined often, looking from Kirk to the shadowy outline of the trail.

At last he came to his feet. He trotted down the trail for a distance of perhaps thirty feet, stopped, and looked back. Again he whined. Finally he barked, loud and long, ending on a note of despair. There was no movement from his master. The dog turned and ran swiftly into the timber in the direction of Camp Three.

VII

TIMBER PIRATES

OUTSIDE the wind howled around the exposed corners of the many-storied building, rattling the windows. Every once in a while the wind unloaded its cargo of snowflakes and in these intervals the husky man at the window could see the ice-lined shore of the lake and the people, as tiny and as futile as ants, huddling the sides of the buildings on the sidewalks of Michigan Boulevard below.

J. P. Schwartz turned his head away from the window as the office flunkey, first knocking, entered bearing an armload of logs which he deposited in the brass kettle near the open fireplace. Schwartz's office boasted a fireplace and its cheery blaze, turning the pine-panelled walls a golden brown, felt good to-day. The fire was unnecessary, for the modern building was equipped with all the latest devices for heating and air conditioning, but Schwartz liked the swanky note it lent his office. He gestured to the janitor, and the latter, a thin, bent-over old man, pushed a leather armchair up alongside the fire. Sprawling in the deep, green cushions, Schwartz drew deeply on the wet end of his dollar cigar and blew the expensive smoke into the chimney. The corner of his pudgy mouth lifted and his sleek, unwrinkled skin creased into a grin. J. P. Schwartz was feeling particularly good that day.

In the first place, the board meeting at noon had been an unqualified success. Of course Schwartz *was* the Great Western Lumber Company, but still it gratified him to have a board of directors; and on a day like the present, when every man had gone out of his way to placate the big boss, Schwartz felt that the twenty-dollar bill each director received for attending the meeting was only a token of his real worth. They had cracked jokes, smoked expensive cigars and imported cigarettes, and later, to the accompaniment of hail and snow blown against the windows, dinner had been served in the board room. Schwartz had had lobster.

Suddenly Schwartz whirled around and stared at the huge map hanging on the wall behind his desk. It was a map of the north-western United States.

Here and there, spotting the white background, were patches of a brilliant red, just as though someone had spattered blood indiscriminately over the map. These were the holdings of the Great Western Lumber Company. Schwartz had noticed that the British Empire was always coloured red on the maps and it had pleased him to have his dominions coloured red also.

Schwartz rose from the comfortable armchair by the fire and seated himself behind the huge mahogany desk, which was spotless and plain except for the file on one corner holding letters and the old silver inkstand in the middle. Despite his pudgy, thick-cheeked face and his broad, imposing figure, Schwartz was not a flabby man. When he walked, he moved quickly with lumbering steps that reminded one of a bear.

Schwartz had started in life as a stevedore on the west coast. It did not take him long to discover that brute strength, which he had in plenty, could force other men to do his will and lighten his labours. But it was not until his first trip away from the coast, a winter spent in logging in the Washington woods, that he discovered that guile, trickery, and brains could work more miracles than mere brute strength. Schwartz had not hesitated to use force after that, but it was his mastery of guile that won him the red-coloured empire covering many thousands of acres.

Taking a small key from his watch chain, Schwartz unlocked a big drawer on the right side of his desk. In the back of the big drawer, cleverly concealed to evade prying eyes, was a smaller, secret drawer. Here Schwartz kept the reports of his agents in the field, crude sheets, badly ruled, written in pencil. Schwartz was too clever a man to use his own organisation in various projects that might not fall within the letter of the law, but he had quite a scattered list of men, hired when he was in his hunting lodge in the North Woods, under his control, willing to do his bidding. So accustomed had he become to using guile, that now he went out of his way to get things by trickery that he could have got by straight dealing. He did not realise it, but this trait of character had made a coward of him.

Reading over one of these crudely written sheets Schwartz suddenly smiled. He reached over and took a red pencil from the silver inkstand, then he rose and faced the map. Adjusting his pince-nez, he found the apple-shaped country almost in the centre of the map. He drew a heavy red line all around the borders of the property. This was the section that Dan Kirk had been cruising, and the heavy red line signified that it was now part of the Schwartz Great Western Lumber Company domain.

Next Schwartz ran a pudgy finger over the borders of Northern Lumber Company's holdings. Again the pencil moved, but this time the line was a thin, broken one. Then, on a spot near the Cranmer River, very close to Camp Three, Schwartz labouriously drew two heavy crosses. He stood back from the map, admiring his handiwork. He could have the section ruled by a heavy coloured line to-morrow.

K

With a sigh of satisfaction, he brushed off his hands, closed the drawer in his desk, and putting on his hat and coat went out the door, shutting it behind him.

Big Jim Healy slogged along through the late afternoon shadows, grumbling because the light harness of the sledge he was dragging cut into his shoulders.

Ahead of him, breaking trail, chunky Wes Read called back over his shoulder, "C'm'on, Jim, quit your crabbin'. We ain't got far to go."

"You been sayin' that all afternoon," the big man returned. "Guess you did enough beefin' when you lugged this thing this morning." Grunting, Healy jerked the toboggan over a snagging spear of brush, and for the moment the conversation was halted. The sledge was loaded with a cooking outfit and tent, axes, surveyor's steel chain, and a transit knocked down in its box. A tripod for the instrument completed the load. They had just finished a three days' stay in the field; the weather had been bitter for such work, and their tempers were on edge.

Read fumbled in the pocket of his mackinaw for a plug of tobacco. Biting off a big chew, he replaced the plug and spat into the snow. The snow crackled and made a popping sound as the tobacco struck it. "Cripes an' it's cold!" Read muttered, beating his mittened hands against his sides. "Well, we've only got about three miles more—and then for a big feed. Keep swingin', Jim."

For perhaps another mile they pushed on in silence. Then Read pulled up short and Healy, plodding along his face to the ground, nearly walked up Read's back. Before Healy could get out more than a muttered oath, he noticed Read's pointing hand and followed the direction it indicated, towards the edge of the clearing they were passing over. "Well, I'll be—— What do you make of that, Wes? A dog!"

"Yeah," Wes replied, his breath expiring in a whistle. "Gave me a scare. I thought it was a wolf."

Spike stood watching the two men from the cover of a clump of brush. His muzzle was grey with frost and he held one foot high as if he sought relief from the cold. The hair along his neck bristled, and he watched the two warily.

Spike trotted out into the open, circling the men, keeping his eyes focused on them intently. At last he came within several yards of where they stood. He stopped and looked straight at them, not moving a muscle.

"Now where the devil did you come from?" queried Healy.

Read watched the dog with admiring eyes. "Cripes, but he's a beauty! Wonder who owns him? Here, boy!" Read squatted on his haunches and held out his hand. Spike merely turned his head slightly and looked distantly at the man. He growled and the growl ended up in a muffled bark. Then he wheeled suddenly and moved off into the timber.

Healy shifted the shoulder harness and snorted at his partner. "There you go, bucko. Got a way with animals, ain't ya? That's the last you'll see of that fellow. How are you with kids?"

Read stood upright, pointing. "Look at him, Jim. He's back. That guy wants something."

Read was right. Spike had vanished momentarily into the brush. His pleading bark had, in his lights, been sufficient to urge the men on. When they failed to respond, he returned to plead with them to follow him. This time he ran swiftly into the open and gave throat to a series of louder barks. He turned and ran towards the timber, then stopped and barked again.

"Something's up, Wes," Healy said. "Let's follow him. Dogs don't act that way for nothin'."

"Better leave the sled here. No use luggin' that thing along."

Healy shook his head, but he quickly slipped the shoulder straps off nevertheless. "No, I'm takin' it along. We can cache the junk here, though; then we can pick it up when we come back. Lend us a hand."

Together they managed to get the gear off the toboggan in a hurry, Spike barking at them all the while. Covering over the instruments with a tarpaulin, the two men hurriedly followed the dog along the trail he had just made. Spike ran on ahead, encouraged now that he had succeeded in attracting their attention. Occasionally he looked over his shoulder as he loped through the drifted snow, but as the men showed no signs of giving up he piloted them straight to where Dan lay in the snow.

Healy was in the lead and the first to notice the huddled figure as they swung down the trail. "Some guy's hurt, Wes," he called out between laboured gasps for breath. "By golly, that darned dog came to get our help."

"Step on it," his friend urged. "He may be bad off."

They knelt beside the stricken Kirk and pulled him over on his back. His back had slipped from its trunk support and he was lying on his side, doubled up, in the snow. One look at the man told the story. His moccasins were coated with ice and his hands inside the mitts were clenched into fists.

"Frozen! Went through the ice and couldn't dry out."

"Is he alive?" Wes wanted to know.

Healy felt Dan's pulse and nodded. From behind them came a snarl, and both men wheeled. Spike was pacing up and down, his head low to the snow, his ears flattened, lips drawn back over white, gleaming fangs.

"Better do something about the dog, Wes," Healy commanded. "We've got to work fast with this guy, and if the dog don't let us touch him we're stuck."

Read turned away and began talking to Spike. He spoke in a low, steady voice which gradually had an effect. Spike's growls became less menacing. As Read talked, Healy was busy. He dragged the toboggan alongside Kirk and rolled him over on to the low sled. With a light lashing line he bound Dan to prevent his sliding off. Then he stood to adjust the shoulder harness.

When he was ready at last, he spoke to Read. "I can handle this load alone, Wes. But we got to move this guy quick if we're not just goin' to bury him.

Tell you what. You go ahead and sort of break trail. Call the dog with you. He'll go along okay as soon as he sees we're bringin' the guy too. Get to the cabin, but don't start a fire. Break open that can of coal oil—and see if there ain't a spot of rum left in the bottle. Get goin', now!"

Calling to Spike, Read struck out ahead. For just a moment the dog hesitated, uncertain, but as Healy eased the sled into motion he seemed to understand what was expected of him. He trotted ahead, though he ran in Read's wake. Keeping an eye peeled over his shoulder, he would wait till Healy caught up to him, then run on ahead until he was behind Read once more. Something deep in the dim consciousness of the dog, some sense that we human beings identify as reason but which is rather an indefinable intuition, told him that Dan was helpless and needed the aid of these men.

So, with the forest becoming as black as midnight, the little party hurried on, Healy labouring like a truck-horse beneath his load, Read breaking trail, and Spike acting as liaison between the two. Occasionally he broke the regularity of his procedure to trot back to the side of the toboggan. There he would walk along looking at Dan's closed eyes and silent figure, barking once or twice as if asking him to speak. Then he would race ahead as though to urge the sweating Nealy on to greater efforts. They passed the pile of equipment, which loomed out of the darkness like a snow-covered boulder, but they did not stop until at last they drew up before a small one-room cabin.

Read, arriving first, had completed preparations. A brilliant gasoline lamp shimmered on the snow through the half-open door and the blankets of one of the two bunks had been turned back. He stepped out of the cabin just as Healy brought the sled to a stop. Together they bent, lifted Dan, and carried him inside.

Sniffing the interior of the room carefully as he followed, Spike then went to the foot of the bed and sat down there watching every move the two men made. They worked swiftly and efficiently, each knowing exactly what was needed if Dan was to be saved. Being the bigger of the two, Healy took charge of handling Dan, lifting him up as Read poured a tin cup full of burning whisky between the closed lips. The warm liquor seemed to revive the lumberman to some extent, but he still drowsed and mumbled as Healy removed his clothes.

Read in the meantime was not idle. From the junk on the shelves he produced a large wash boiler and two small tin basins. Into these he poured the entire contents of a five-gallon can of kerosene. This done, he helped his partner shift Kirk so that he lay crosswise on the bunk, his feet hanging down towards the floor. Heavy blankets were thrown over Dan's upper body. Then his feet were set into the wash boiler and each hand placed in a basin of oil resting on either side of the man. They examined the extent of progress made by the frost. One foot was frozen almost to the ankle, while the frost line on the other stopped at the instep. The fingers of both hands had been touched, one up to the wrist.

"Just got him in time," Healy muttered. "I think we can pull the frost. Don't seem to be too deep for the coal oil to work on. . . . How 'bout gettin' some grub?"

"Don't want to heat the place up yet, do you? Better keep it a bit chilly till that stuff starts to work."

Healy scoffed at the suggestion. "You're an awful dumbbell, Wes," he answered impatiently. "Of course we ain't goin' to heat the place. Sling a blanket from the rafter so's it drops in front of the stove—and don't set too much of a fire. That'll keep the heat from this side of the room. I'll get something for the dog. He sure deserves it."

While Read arranged the blanket around the stove in the far corner of the cabin and made preparations for supper, Healy went outside and took down a quarter of deer meat from a pole sling arched across the roof. It was frozen stiff, but he managed to chop off several steaks with the axe. Three of these he tossed on the table for Wes to prepare for supper. The largest cut he held out to Spike.

The dog ignored it. He rose to his haunches, stretched his head towards the meat, but he refused to budge from a sitting position despite the entreaties of the stranger. His nose quivered with impatience, but he would not eat from hand. Healy grinned understandingly. He took out a pocket-knife and shredded the hard meat into a pan. This he set on the floor in front of the dog. Spike looked at him, satisfied himself that he was not going to be interfered with, and advanced to the plate. The meat did not last long. He licked the platter clean and explored the floor around it before returning to his place at the foot of the bunk.

Dan remained in a coma for over an hour. Every once in a while he moved or muttered a little and several times he tried to withdraw his feet or his hands from the oil, but each time Healy carefully replaced the frozen members.

Read hurried with the meal, and soon hot venison steaks, bread, coffee, and beans were on the table. The two sat down to eat.

"Think it's gettin' too hot in here, Jim?" Read asked as he helped himself to a husky slab of meat.

The other shook his head. "That oil has started to work and it don't matter now if it does warm up a bit."

"How long does it take to draw the frost?"

Healy speared a piece of bread with his fork and shrugged his shoulders in a gesture of helplessness. "How do I know? Depends on how bad it is. . . . Say, what do you make of this guy anyhow?"

"Must be one from of the camps. Don't seem to be a brush rat, though."

"No jack would be wanderin' around up here when there's sticks to be cut. Looks like some kind of a straw boss to me. Better take it easy when he comes to. We've got to find out what he's doin' up here."

They had finished their meal and were cleaning up the dishes when Dan gave positive evidence of coming around. His eyes opened and for some minutes he lay there, staring up at the rough log ceiling and thinking for a while he was in his own bed. Trying to move his hands, he realised for the first time that they were both immersed in basins. He looked around the room and saw nothing familiar. Hearing low voices behind the blanket, he called out weakly, "Hey, there. Where am I?"

Spike came to his feet at the sound of his master's voice. He put his feet up on the side of the bunk and looked at the prone figure, his big tail waving wildly and a low whine escaping from between his clenched jaws. He lifted his head and gave vent to a sharp, quick bark—a sign of his joy.

Healy came from behind the blanket, a dirty dish towel slung across his shoulders. "You're okay, pardner. Just take it easy now and keep your hands and feet where they are. You've had a close shave with that frost, but I think we've got it beat now."

Healy sat down on the edge of the bed and examined Dan's hands, nodding his head as he did so. Stooping over, he looked at each of the feet. "Unh-huh," he said, grunting as he seated himself again. "Yes, sir, we've got it licked. But it was close, mister. And you can thank your lucky stars and your friend here for gettin' you out in time. He sure made a nuisance of himself till he got us to follow him. What happened any way?"

Gradually the sequence of the day's events came back to Dan and he told how, foolishly, he had gone through the ice. He explained about his having only one match and how Spike had flicked snow on the fire just as it was well started. "I tried to keep going," he concluded, "but somehow my feet just wouldn't move. Then I leaned up against a stump and tried to remember not to fall asleep . . . and from then on I was out. I can't recall a thing."

Read came from behind the curtain at last and stood beside the bed, listening to the recital. "Well, if the dog was to blame, he sure made up for it," he commented. "It was darn near human, him comin' up to us and tryin' to tell us something was wrong. And was he mad when he saw us messin' around. Liked to take a hunk out of our hides. Glad he didn't —might have poisoned a good dog," he said, laughing. "Where'd you get him?"

Before Dan could answer, Spike made his presence known again. Impatient at his master's delay in recognising him, he circled the bunk and carefully crawled up beside Dan on the side opposite the wash-tub. He moved with great caution, careful not to upset the basins, and snuggled down beside Dan, his red tongue wetting the man's neck. Soft whimpers of happiness came from him as he sensed that Dan was once more the master whom he had grown to love and who had been so strangely silent through these last hours. Healy and Read laughed and slapped their sides at the dog's actions.

"You sure got yourself a dog, stranger, and no mistake," Big Jim said. "Now how 'bout some grub?"

"I could eat," Dan replied. "How bad are these frostbites of mine?"

"Just bad enough to lay you up for a spell, that's all," Read explained.

Going to the stove, Healy took down the blanket, then prepared a plate of food for Kirk. "That oil sure does the trick," he said. "There won't be any cutting off of toes this trip. Another few minutes, though, and the chill would have got into the bone; then it would've been just too bad."

As he ate and drank, Dan kept wondering who these men were who had befriended him and what their business was. Hart had said nothing on his last trip in about any other men out here. Evidently the same question was bothering Healy and Read too, for as they seated themselves near the bed and produced pipes, Healy casually inquired, "You with Northern Lumber?"

Kirk nodded, his mouth full of food.

"What camp you out of?" Healy persisted.

"I went in with the gang at Camp Two," Dan replied.

"That's Hart's gang, ain't it " Read asked.

Dan nodded again. The other two exchanged glances carefully, glances Dan did not see since he had his nose buried in a steaming hot cup of coffee. As Read lowered the cup, he continued, "Yes, that's the gang I came in with. However, I've been floating around here most of the winter—looking timber on this property."

The next question took Kirk completely off guard.

"Know Bart McQuade?" Healy inquired.

Startled, his eyes wide, Kirk looked up quickly. Luckily the other two had their eyes averted, watching Spike. Why on earth should these two men mention McQuade's name in connection with Hart? The unspoken question left him uneasy. He lowered his eyes and answered in an even tone.

"Yes. Slightly. Why? Do you know him?"

"Unh-huh." Healy leaned over so that his elbows rested on his knees. He pared his nails with the small blade of his jackknife while Read sat with arms folded silently watching both of them. "Yeah, we know Bart. Good timberman, that fellow . . . What'd you say your name was, mister?"

"I don't recall saying, but it's Kirk—Dan Kirk." Dan was becoming just a bit annoyed at the inquisitiveness of his hosts. Besides, his hands and feet were beginning to ache.

He mentioned the fact to Healy—about the ache —and the big man snapped his knife shut and gave the injured members a thorough inspection. "Guess we can take them out of the oil now. The frost seems to be all drawn out. Get a towel, Wes."

Healy carefully mopped up the oil and straightened Dan so that he lay properly in the bunk. A big fire was built up, since it was impossible for Dan to stand the weight of the blankets on his feet. After a while the other two made ready for bed, Healy taking the other bunk while Read prepared to bed down on the floor.

"You'll have to stick around for a few days, Kirk," Healy said as he turned the light out. He went on to explain, "Don't want to risk those hands and feet for a spell. . . . But we'll take good care of you, eh, Wes?"

Out of the dark came a muffled, indistinguishable reply.

Spike's cold nose lay against Dan's cheek and an exploring tongue licked his neck. He had refused to leave the man and had stretched out beside him, one paw braced against Dan's chest. Somehow Dan could not get to sleep. For one thing, the blood pounding back into the frostbitten hands and feet set them burning like fire. For another, and this was the main reason, he could not come to a satisfactory conclusion about the identity of Healy and Read. What were they doing out here? Clearly they did not belong to any of the other camps of Northern Lumber. Had there been any other cruisers on the job, Hart would certainly have mentioned it. Of course they might be State men running survey lines—Dan had noticed the transit which Read brought in before they went to bed. Or again they might be cruisers from some other outfit bent on the same mission as himself.

This last conclusion seemed to be the only logical answer, but it was not likely that in that event they should have been so secretive about themselves. Dan had purposely refrained from questioning them, and now he decided to bide his time and permit Healy and Read the chance of explaining themselves and their presence in the timber, far from any of the camps. But somehow their interest in him, and also in Hart and McQuade, stirred a vague sense of uneasiness within him, and he felt that the whole situation had an unhealthy smell about it.

Dan was forced to remain in bed for nearly two weeks. During that time Spike never left the side of the bunk except to eat and take a daily short run around the cabin. Dan amused himself by reading the few dime novels and magazines the cabin boasted or by playing pinochle with his hosts. The two men seemed to have lost all interest in whatever work they were commissioned to do and they, too, stayed close to the cabin. Never once, although Dan often steered the conversation that way, did they offer any explanation of their connection with any company. They simply said they were doing a little survey work and let it go at that.

The time came when Dan could stir about. For the first two or three days he contented himself with short walks in the vicinity of the cabin. His feet were still tender and his hands itched considerably. Aside from that he felt no ill effects from his experience. But he was beginning to feel uneasy about getting back to his own cabin. There was still a good bit of work to be done if he expected to finish his estimates by spring.

One morning after breakfast, while the three of them were still sitting around the rude table, Dan announced his intention of leaving. "I've been imposing on you fellows long enough," he said easily, pushing his coffee cup away. "It's about time Spike and I hit the trail." He got up, stretched, and went to the hooks that served as clothes hangers.

Healy had been sitting across the table from Dan, while Read had just started to get up and stack the dishes. The two of them quickly acted as though they were given a signal. Wes Read stepped quickly to the door and stood with his back against it. Healy, moving surprisingly fast for such a big man, reached his own bunk in two steps and slipped a huge revolver from underneath his blankets.

"You'd better change your mind, Kirk," Healy said, levelling the pistol at Dan's back. His voice was cold and curt and his eyes narrowed to slits, a vivid contrast to his usual cheery, easy-going manner.

Dan turned around, then started in surprise as he saw the gun in Healy's hand. Completely puzzled at the turn of events, he stood there holding his mackinaw in his hand, looking from one to the other. "What's the big idea, Healy?" he asked finally. "Are you in the habit of kidnapping people?"

"We don't intend to have any one go home squealin' about us being here, not till we get ready to leave. You're stayin', Kirk, so sit down."

Dan looked straight at the man. There was no compromise in those hard, dark eyes. Spike came to Kirk and sniffed his pant leg, then looked at Healy and growled. Dan threw his coat on the bed and resumed his seat at the table, and Spike came and sat beside him.

though not understand, on the sound of the footfall, had left the cabin a little. They were thus quite sure who it was; even that had penetrated.

VIII

SPRING DRIVE

"I'D advise you to put up that gun, Healy," Dan said, speaking in an even tone, his eyes held steadily on those of the bigger man.

It was a curious picture, this tableau being enacted in the little cabin miles away from anywhere, and Dan did not care overmuch for the part assigned to him. For five minutes the other two had been like figures in a waxworks, not moving and not speaking. Evidently they had been unprepared to face Dan's decision to leave and their sudden resolve to act, though not undertaken on the spur of the moment, had left them out on a limb. They were not quite sure what to do from that point on. As Dan spoke, Read moved uneasily at his position by the door, but Kirk kept his eyes riveted on Healy.

Healy smiled a crooked grin that transformed his placid face into a sneering caricature of itself. He balanced the revolver easily in his hand. "I'm givin' orders around here, Mr. Kirk," he replied.

The thing that struck Dan most forcibly was the rapid change which had suddenly come over the man, the quick transition from a hulking, good-natured giant to a ruthless, calculating scoundrel who, Kirk was sure, would not hesitate a single minute to pull the trigger if he so much as made a false move. Read was only a weakling, influenced by the stronger Healy, but dangerous in his weakness just the same. Dan squirmed in his chair, stalling for time. His hand dropped to the bristling scruff of Spike's neck. The dog sat still beside him, stirring uneasily, perplexed by the peculiar actions of the men he had become used to.

Healy spoke again. "I'll do all the talkin' from now on, see? We knew from the day we brought you in that you wasn't wanderin' around up here in the snow for your health. Spyin' don't pay, Mr. Kirk, and now that you found what you're lookin' for, we don't intend to let you go back and spill your insides to the wrong party."

"Spying!" Dan's surprise was genuine. "I'm not spying on you. Do you think I'd go out and nearly freeze to death right where you could find me if that was the case?" He paused for a moment to let his question sink home. Almost casually he added: "Besides, what is there to spy on?"

The chance question scored a hit. Realising he had said too much, Healy's face flushed, and suddenly he lost some of the cruel lines on his face, regaining a little of his ordinary placid appearance.

Read stirred and put in a hurried, albeit lame, explanation. "Jim didn't mean that. It's just that we was doin' some work up here and you came along, and . . . well, interrupted us, and we aim to find out what your business is."

Dan looked from one to the other. He had wondered from the first just what these two were doing, snugly quartered here among the big sticks in the dead of winter, far away from any of the lumber camps. And now Healy's inadvertant mention of spying was surely an admission of guilt—guilt of what? Kirk's mind worked fast as he tried to piece the thing together. For the life of him Kirk could not think of anything the men were doing that might harm Northern Lumber Company. Only one thing was certain. They were on a mission that they desperately wanted to keep secret—so much so that they had resorted to force in order to keep him a prisoner. Force and secrecy, combined with the fact that Hart had mentioned Schwartz's interest in the property, spelled just one thing to Dan—the Great Western Lumber Company. If Read and Healy had been merely rival cruisers, they would have been above-board, friendly; they could have nothing to hide, even if they were looking the timber over for

Great Western. Dan's course was clear. He must play for a chance to outwit them, and then get to Hart with the information. He had not talked to Hart in over two months. A lot could have happened in that time.

His glance dropped until it rested on Spike, and carelessly he stroked the dog's head as if resigned to the fact that he was beaten. Spike trod from one forefoot to the other as he looked up at his master, pressing his head against Dan's hand in a plea for more petting. Stealthily Kirk glanced at Healy from beneath lowered lids. The big man still seemed confused over the break he had made. The barrel of the pistol pointed towards the floor, out of the direct line to Dan's mid-section.

"You win," Kirk said at last, smiling and throwing up his hands in a gesture of futility. "I'll be darned if I know what it's all about, but you've got the drop on me, that's a cinch. What do I do now?"

Healy gave a sigh that sounded very much like a gasp of relief and seated himself at the table. Resting the pistol on the table with the business end still pointing at Dan's stomach, Healy poured himself another cup of coffee with his left hand. "Just follow orders and stick around," he replied. "As long as you stick near the cabin and don't try to make a getaway, everything'll be jake. It won't be long before the spring thaw sets in, and after that we don't care what you do. But right now it's better for all concerned that nobody knows about me and Wes here. And just to make sure you don't walk out on us we'll remove some of your clothes. Wes, take the gentleman's moccasins and mackinaw. Mitts, too. Can't travel far up here half naked."

But while Healy had been talking, Dan had been doing some quick thinking. Unnoticed by the other two, he had hunched himself in the chair until he was like a coiled spring, his body leaning forward, his legs bunched up and braced beneath the chair. As Read stepped away from the door to carry out Healy's instructions, Dan seized the ruff of fur around the dog's neck and shoved Spike in his path, at the same time shouting at the top of his voice, "Get 'em, Spike—get 'em!" He counted on the psychological effect of the shouting to confuse Read more than the dog's rush.

Kirk moved so fast then that the events of the next few minutes were lost in a blur of sound and action. As he pushed Spike, he lifted the edge of the table with his right hand and pushed simultaneously with his knees. It was a desperate chance, but it worked. The other edge of the table struck Healy's knees and knocked him forward; both Healy and the table described arcs in mid-air that met with a crack as loud as a pistol shot. The gun flew out of Healy's hand over his shoulder and the chair slipped from beneath him. In a second Dan was on his feet. He heard a vicious roar from Spike and a scream of pain from Read. He was too busy to look, for at that moment he sent his fist crashing against Healy's jaw, just as the surprised giant, none the worse for his crack on the head, was rising to his feet. The full impact of the blow toppled the big man against the shelves, and he sat down again.

Quickly Dan whirled around and picked up the pistol. Covering Healy, he called to Spike. "Down, Spike—down, boy! Here now!"

Raging with excitement, Spike stood snarling over the prostrate form of Read, who, with one arm uplifted to protect his face from the dog's fury, was scrambling backwards on the floor as fast as he could go.

"Here, boy. Come here. Shut up, Read. He won't hurt you."

Spike, hearing Dan's voice, looked at him over his shoulder, undecided what was expected of him next. He had acted purely from impulse. When Dan pushed him, his natural reaction was to attack the oncoming Read. Now his master spoke to him in the steady voice he used to command obedience. Slowly Spike retreated, sniffing first at Read and then at Healy, who sat with his hands slightly raised, bewilderment, fear, and hatred smouldering in his eyes as a thin trickle of blood curved down his chin. Spike returned to Dan's side and rested on his haunches.

Dan smiled—a peculiar smile that barely lifted the corners of his mouth. "Now it's my turn to do the talking. I don't know what you two are up to, but whatever it is it stinks to high heaven. I'm not taking any chances till I find out, and I can't lug both of you along with me to camp—although Hart probably knows you and would be tickled pink to see you again. So, we'll just have to fix a place for you here where you can be out of the way while I'm getting into camp. After that we'll be ready for anything you want to pull. . . . Sit still now, Healy. Keep reaching."

Slung from a wall peg was a coil of light line of the type used for lashing a sledge load. Keeping the gun on the two men, Kirk unhitched the coil and shook out the rope with one hand. Holding the butcher knife braced against his body and the make-shift sink, he cut the rope in two. This done, he spoke to Healy. "Stand up. And keep your hands raised."

"You ain't gettin' away with anything," Healy snarled.

"Let me be the judge of that."

Dan took him by the arm and whirled him around so that he faced the wall. Twisting the end of the rope into a noose, Dan reached up and slipped it over Healy's wrist. "Now lower that other hand and please don't try anything funny." He bound the man's two wrists securely behind his back.

Dan sat Healy on the edge of the bunk, then went to work on Read. In a few minutes they were both trussed up, helpless, and Dan replaced the gun on the table. He laughed. "Unfortunately it's you two who are going to stick around for a while. Sit down on the floor—both of you—one at each end of the bunk. Come on, move!"

With much grumbling and swearing, Read and Healy tumbled to the floor, their backs against the solid posts of the bunk, which were secured both to the floor and to one of the rafters of the cabin. Then Dan lashed their arms and legs so that they could not budge an inch.

"I'll get you for this, Kirk. I'll get you for it if it takes the rest of my life," Healy sputtered. He had lost the look of placid bewilderment and now his face was red with rage. Read was morose ; he had not uttered a word since Dan had called off Spike.

Dan rose to his knees and surveyed the job. Satisfied, he poured out a bucket of water and placed both the bucket and a tin cup within easy reach of the men. "You'll be able to wiggle out of those knots—after a while," he said, smiling down at the two. "You may get a little hungry, but you'll enjoy your grub more when you get to it."

Remembering the need that had been the cause of his leaving his own cabin, Dan made up a pack of several deer steaks, some salt, some tea, and a small pan for heating water. He put on his mackinaw and drew on his mitts and, first breaking it open and withdrawing the cartridges, slipped the pistol into a side pocket. His hand on the latch of the door, he turned and faced the trussed men. "So long, boys. Thanks for what you did for me. I'm sorry I couldn't show my gratitude in a better way. . . . Come along, Spike." He held the door open and the dog glided out, eager to be in the open.

Dan stepped outside and closed the door. He set off at a rapid pace at a tangent to the direction in which his own cabin lay, but he hoped to hit the surveying trail, thus saving time in the long run. The snow had melted somewhat, then hardened again, forming a crust through which he constantly broke. It was difficult going; inside of an hour his still tender feet commenced to ache. This only made him **try** the harder to keep up a quick, steady pace.

He tried to get the whole puzzling situation **clear** in his mind as he walked along, plunging through the crusted snow. The only conclusion that would make sense was the inescapable one that he was once again involved in some kind of timber piracy of the kind that had ruined his father and himself. It seemed to him that the fine Italian hand of the Great Western Lumber Company was lurking somewhere in the background, and that he needed only one or two facts to bring it out clearly in the light. But the thing that puzzled Dan most was how two men could possibly do any damage to Northern Lumber. Why did Healy and Read attempt to detain him by force? How far advanced were the plans, if any, to swing a crushing blow against Northern? Evidence of outside influence would have been plain had there been any gangs up in the property he was cruising, gangs cutting timber; or even if there had been labour trouble in any of Northern's own camps. . . . Labour trouble! Wasn't there a connection in that? Healy had seemed to be particularly interested in McQuade. Hadn't he spoken of him in rather glowing terms? Even Hart had said that he knew nothing whatsoever about Bart except that the big fellow was a first-rate logger. And McQuade was just the sort of braggart who felt that his rewards never equalled his deserts, and who, therefore, could be bought easily by a rival company to foment trouble. Then McQuade was due in Camp Three about this time. It all seemed to add up somehow.

The more he thought the more apprehensive he became, until finally he was practically trotting down the trail.

Had it not been for his timber estimates, still remaining in the cabin, Dan would have headed immediately for Camp Three; but he hated to see a winter's work thrown to nothing, for there was no telling what might happen to them now if Great Western was really on the rampage. He still had a week's cruising left to complete the job, but that seemed unimportant compared with the recent developments. The spring thaw was fast approaching and the river ice might go out any day. If there was going to be an attempt to delay Northern's drive of logs, it would certainly happen soon. At any rate, Dan consoled himself, Read and Healy could not loosen their bonds before Dan had time to get back to camp.

As the day advanced and the going became if anything increasingly difficult, Spike walked along beside his master in a manner that was strange to him. Instead of racing ahead, as he so often did when they were out together, he held himself in check, and he kept constantly tossing his head over his shoulder to watch Dan. At times he walked so close to the man that Dan had to urge him on to keep from stumbling against him. It was as though the dog understood the events in the past that had overpowered his master and made him helpless, and that he sought to offer what help he could to prevent their recurrence.

Night came swiftly, and it was completely dark,

without a star in the sky, by the time they reached the cabin. Dan's feet were dreadfully sore. The tenderness had not yet left them and the constant breaking through the hard crust had battered them more than he realised. His hands were swollen and sore, too, from the pounding of the blood in them all day long; they were puffed up in an ugly fashion. He lighted the lamp and started a fire in the stove. They had Healy's steaks for supper, and soon Spike, well fed, lay by the stove cleaning his pads. Dan rolled up his maps, charts, and figures and placed them in the pack he had made in the morning. His plan was to rest for a few hours, then push on to Camp Three over the easily followed surveyors' route. He removed his boots and stretched out on the bunk, pipe in mouth. In a few minutes he became drowsy and put the pipe aside. Before he knew it he had passed into a deep, exhausted slumber.

It was cold in the cabin when he awoke. He tried to sit up, but the effort sent a spasm of pain shooting up both his thighs. His feet were swollen and throbbed regularly like the pulsating beat of a giant engine; his puffed hands ached all the way to his shoulders. He hunched his body till his feet touched the floor, and bending over he tried to slip his boots on. It was no use; his feet were too swollen. He tried to stand, but he quickly had to sit down again. He could not even bear his own weight. Sitting on the edge of the bunk, he reached over and grasped Spike's head in his arms. Spike had aroused when his master first stirred and had trotted over immediately to sit and watch him. "Well, mister," Dan said, addressing his pet, "this is a fine how-do-you-do. Here we've got a long hike ahead of us and I can't even get my shoes on. . . . It's starting to thaw, too. The ice may go out in the next twenty-four hours. Lord, but I hope that rope is strong; I don't give a good darn if Healy and Read do starve."

But if Dan had set his hopes on being able to start in the morning, he was to be sadly disappointed. It was agony for him to move as far as the stove, and for three days he had difficulty even in preparing food for Spike and himself.

To make matters worse, the thaw continued. Spring was in the country at last. Lying in his bunk one night with Spike crouched beside him, and silently cursing his luck, he heard a distant rolling roar like the boom of far-off surf. "There she goes," he said aloud. "That's the ice in the Cranmer. And here we sit without raisin' a hand. Fellow, we're shoving off to-morrow if I have to crawl."

Later that night it started to rain. For hours the rain came down in solid sheets, flushing off the snow and loosening torrents into the rivers. The boom of the white water rose higher in volume as the man sat cursing the luck that held him housebound when forces were at work that might mean the ruin of the company employing him, the loss of hundreds of thousands of dollars, and perhaps the lives of many splendid loggers.

The next morning the rain had let up somewhat and Dan made ready to leave. He packed a small shelter tent and enough provisions for three days. Regardless of the urgency of his journey, he would have to take the trip in easy stages if he intended to reach Camp Three at all. With everything ready at last, his gun and extra clothing under lock and key, his reports wrapped carefully in oilskins and secure in the pack across his shoulders, Kirk closed the door of the little cabin that had been his home for so many months. With Spike laughing at his side, happy to be out despite the rain, Dan set out for Camp Three.

Spike continued to act peculiarly on the trip home. Before when they had gone afield, it had been Spike's joy to race ahead, flushing game, crashing through small by-streams, and hiding from Dan to leap out at him unawares. Perhaps it was the freezing incident that had changed Spike's viewpoint. At any rate he acted now as he had done when they were coming from Healy's cabin, refusing to leave Dan's side on any account. At times when the trail narrowed he would trot a few feet ahead, but usually he preferred to be at the man's side, pressing his strong body against Dan's legs. He seemed to feel that it was through his negligence that his master had come to grief, and he was not taking any chances on its happening again.

Dan did not head straight for the Cranmer. The place where he had crossed before on the ice would now be a raging torrent, worth any man's life to ford. Instead he headed back for a couple of miles to a spot where a small island in the middle of the river forked the stream into two swift-moving rapids. Here, anticipating such a need, Dan had felled two massive trees. Even though the water was high, he could cross with comparative safety on these. After he had crossed the river—and it was over an hour from the time of leaving before he did so—the going was easier. The rain let up and gradually the sky cleared. When they struck the wide survey lines, several miles below the crossing, the way actually seemed comfortable, although the underbrush was wet and clingy and the ground underfoot soggy. Dan was wearing rubber boots which gave his feet much better protection than the light, flexible moccasins.

At noon they stopped for a quick lunch on cold jerked deer meat. Somewhat refreshed, Dan got under way again, heading due south until it was too dark to see the path. He set up camp in the middle of the trail. After a supper of beans for himself and meat for the dog, Dan crawled into the little tent with Spike wiggling close beside him. They slept till an hour before dawn, ate, struck camp, and were under way long before the lazy sun reached the top of the trees.

About noon they reached a spot in the trail where the Cranmer, taking a wide sweep to the west, came within a mile or so of the Swift. Even above the roar of the Cranmer came the thunderous roll of the Swift, like the booming of the bass in a symphony. Here a small offshoot of the Cranmer meandered lazily off and joined the Swift. That is, it had the last time Dan had seen it. Now it was a raging torrent, swollen to five times its usual size, ranging over rock and tree without regard to any boundaries. Trying to figure out how to cross the stream without

getting a thorough soaking and thus having to take
up precious time drying out, Dan pursued the course
of the stream towards the Swift. Suddenly Dan
pulled up short. He reached down and clutched
Spike's heavy fur. For a minute he stood there
motionless, the dog looking up at him questioningly.
Above the steady roar of the rivers, the baritone of
the Cranmer and the bass of the Swift, came other
sounds—the strident call of men's voices. This was
entirely out of order. As he faced the Swift, Dan
knew that Camp Four was far to his right, on the
other side of the Swift. The crews there would be
busy getting ready for their drive; they couldn't
possibly be in this district. To his left, at the junction
of the Swift and the Cranmer would be Camp Three,
his destination, whose limits also hardly reached
this far up the Cranmer. Who, then, could be active
along this branch, midway between the two camps?
Holding Spike, Dan advanced cautiously in the thick
growth, ankle deep in the swirling waters of the
little stream. He came to a spot where the underbrush suddenly stopped. Peering out, Dan noticed
that here the stream widened till it formed a small
lake. In the clearing along the banks were perhaps
a dozen jacks, feverishly working with peaveys,
tailing down logs to the edge of the stream from a
stock pile about fifty yards from the water's edge.

Standing in the middle of the sweating men, hands
on hips, shouting orders in a bull-like roar, was big
Jim Healy. Instantly the picture was clear to Dan,
like a mirror clearing of steam—the reason for this
scene taking place before him as well as the events

of the past. Somehow, in some devious way, a foreign crew—Great Western's, no doubt—had got between Northern's two camps and had cut logs along this little stream. Not many logs, only a few thousand feet perhaps, but enough for the purpose they were to serve. This had probably been done during the summer, when men in this district were as rare as snow in southern California. The plan was as clear to Dan as Healy's big figure down by the stream. They were going to drive these logs down the flooded stream to crash into the main drive along the Swift. If they were successful, disaster was sure to be the result. It would be like two streams of traffic composed of cars travelling at top speed meeting at right angles. Only the cars would be hundreds of thousands of logs, and the drivers would be Northern's jacks, whose lives, even under the best conditions, were in danger every second they rode the drive. Healy would send his drive down the minute Hart's got under way. Then would come a tremendous jam in the Swift—logs piled up mountain high, men hurt or killed, and the river backing up and flooding the country for miles.

And if it were impossible to break the jam! That meant that Northern would be unable to get their three million feet of timber to the mill in time for market. That in turn meant they would be unable to pay their men and fulfil their contracts. With banks likely to refuse loans, they were then ripe meat for any trifling offer from a rival concern. This was the ace card in the bag of tricks employed by the selfish big interests to freeze out their smaller competitors. There was one, and only one way to stop it. Hart's drive must be held up at any cost. And if possible Camp Four's drive should be stopped too. If the drive could be checked until Healy and his gang were taken care of, the danger would be averted. But by all means the Swift River drive must not go on.

Immediately Dan turned and hurried up the edge of the water. He was determined to reach Camp Three that afternoon if he had to run all the way. Near where the Cranmer roared by, feeding the small stream, Dan sat down and removed his packs and socks. Then he rid himself of everything that would impede his progress—tent, mackinaw, Healy's revolver, food, and cooking utensils. He hid these in a clump of brush and kept only his reports, shoes and socks, and a heavy sweater in the pack which he strapped to his back. Without a moment's hesitation he plunged into the swirling stream. When the icy water was waist high he struck out for the opposite shore. Spike gave a little whimper and followed his master.

As he expected, he was washed several hundred yards downstream, fortunately not quite across from the point where the foreign gang was working. Stopping only a minute to wring out his heavy pants and flannel shirt, he quickly put on socks and shoes, covered his still damp shirt with the heavy sweater, and slung over his shoulder the pack, which seemed light despite its sogginess. Spike shook himself violently two or three times and he was ready. Together they set off at a trot down the Cranmer.

M

A half a mile or so down the Cranmer, Dan came across another pile of logs. Evidently Healy's gang planned to send these down the Cranmer as they were sending the others down the Swift. However, no one was working here, and Dan stopped only long enough to note the fact. From this point Dan headed diagonally across country in order to reach Camp Three.

It was dark when he came in sight of the Swift, but the moon broke clear and white over the trees on the opposite bank. Still travelling at a dog-trot, the breath pounding hot in his chest, Dan prayed that the drive had not started. He could hear nothing that indicated it had—only the ceaseless soughing rush of the big river. He struggled over the rough trail to get down closer to the bank, and as he and Spike stood panting there in the moonlight, he heaved a grateful sigh, for there was not a log floating on the surface of the river. Then, as if by magic, out of the half-light that wrapped the surrounding forests in a cloak of mystery, came a distant, tell-tale sound, and Dan's heart skipped a beat as he stood there looking up the river. Somewhere up the Swift the drive had started.

"Come on, Spike," Dan yelled. Breaking into a run, he crashed through the underbrush towards the camp. With a short bark at the silent, flowing river Spike leaped after his master.

With a roll like the muffled beat of a funeral drum, came the first of the logs, the advance guard of the drive. Bobbing, skidding, plunging, they slipped anxiously through the water, seeking the end of their journey. Others came, and others, until the whole river heaved like a great, dark brown carpet, and the grinding sound as they bumped together and slid over each other grew into a screech of destruction.

Spike stopped and barked futilely at the unaccustomed sight. But as Dan did not halt his stride, the dog went bounding after him.

In ten minutes they were at Camp Three. It was nearly deserted except for Rusty Davis, who was cookee for Camp Three, and young Doyle, a blacksmith helper. They were sitting in the mess shanty over a cup of coffee when Dan and Spike plunged through the door.

"Where's Hart?" Dan demanded breathlessly.

Rusty looked at Dan, his mouth gaping open, his cup raised and held in mid-air. Seeming to come to, he dropped his cup and spoke at the same time. "Hiya, Dan. Upriver with the drive. What's up?"

"Just this—all hell's broke loose. You, Doyle, snap to it. Get up river and find Hart. Get him! And get him in a hurry. Tell him some gang's going to send a drive crashing into the Swift. Tell him Kirk just came in and saw 'em getting ready. Get him to take a gang on up river and stop that outfit. I'll take charge here on the Cranmer, but if he doesn't stop that gang upstream, why. . . . Get going, now! Pronto! . . . How 'bout some grub, Rusty? Quick."

As Doyle leaped for the door, Rusty hustled into the kitchen. He was back in a moment with a plate of steaming food and fresh coffee.

As he bolted his food, Kirk asked. "Where's McQuade and his hunky pal? Do you know?"

Rusty nodded. "Tending out downstream."

"Tending out, eh? I'll bet that so-and-so talked Hart into giving him that job."

This further evidence dovetailed into the picture perfectly. With McQuade and his pal "tending out" —the delicate and important job of watching at river bends and small bayous along the main stream where logs would cluster and form jams—the work of Healy's gang would be simplified. Once the rush of logs down the Cranmer struck the main drive, the men tending out below the junction of the Swift and the Cranmer would do their bit by forming small blockades. Then the big pile-up would come.

Dan gulped his coffee and hurried to the door. Down in Hart's cabin he hastily changed his rubber shoes for spiked driving boots, wearing a pair of Hart's since his feet were swollen again and he could not get his own on. At the blacksmith shop he picked up a peavey, then with Spike bouncing along excitedly by his side hurried on downstream.

The logs were still moving on the Swift, although now they were flowing in a deadly slow steady procession, closely packed from shore to shore. He picked up a crew on the way, curtly ordering, "Drop that. I've got other work for you." They dropped without question, though wondering what was up.

The situation at the junction of the Swift and Cranmer was less satisfactory. Pushing ahead, Dan saw a pile of logs in midstream, several hundred yards from the point where the Cranmer added its turbulent waters to the muddy Swift. The farther they walked the higher grew the pile. Evidently

Healy's gang had released the drive on the Cranmer first, not trusting entirely in their drive on to the Swift to do a thorough job. He could hear the complaining grind of the twenty-four-foot-long sticks as they surged and pressed and groaned but could not advance. Dan hurried along until he reached a point below the ever-rising, already mountainous high, pile of logs.

Out on the calm water below the towering dam of logs, balancing themselves on the strays, were two shadowy figures. At the distance Dan could not be sure, but he thought he recognised McQuade's bulk in one of them. Whatever the two men were doing, it was evident they were not making an attempt to undo the jam.

"Here we are, boys," Dan called, throwing his jacket down on the bank. In a few terse words he presented the situation to the jacks, explaining the paramount importance of breaking that jam and breaking it in a hurry, so that even if Healy started his drive on the Swift they would have an even chance at keeping the logs moving. "And remember," he concluded, "if we don't break this jam quick, we don't eat this year, and maybe we don't work the next."

As Dan leaped nimbly out on the few bobbing logs near shore that had evaded the jam, Spike ran after him and barked. The dog ran to the bank of the river and stood there, his haunches tensely gathered beneath him, quivering, giving vent to a series of loud, persistent barks. The deep-throated bark seemed to carry a warning note.

"Back, Spike. Stay there, boy," Dan called out.

Remaining on the slippery logs, not to mention dancing on them, was more of a gruelling task than Dan had anticipated. He had good reason to curse the thoughtlessness that had led him to acquire a pair of clumsy, frostbitten feet.

As Dan made his way to the centre of the river over the slippery footing, he recognised in the moonlight the red and black wool shirt that was McQuade's uniform. He could not make out what the big fellow was doing, except that he seemed to be rounding up the stray logs and attempting to drive them to the opposite bank, where Dan could barely make out the dim figure of his pal. Because of the shadow from the trees on the edge of the river, McQuade did not notice Dan.

"Hey, McQuade! What do you think you're doin'?"

So startled was the big fellow at the unexpected shout that he slipped and nearly tumbled from his insecure perch. In a moment he had leaped to Dan's side.

"Tryin' to find the centre. What's it to you, grandpa?" Even in the moonlight Dan could see the black look of utter hatred on his face.

"You're going about it in a funny way. Cut to shore."

For a moment rebellion flashed in McQuade's eyes. He started to raise the peavey to swing it above his head when Dan spoke again. "Remember what happened last time. Now get to shore."

Behind Dan, the cornered logger saw the other racing jacks dancing out of the shadows to tackle the jam. His hand fell to his side, and with a look of contempt at Dan, he made his way to shore, paying no attention to the calls and queries of the jacks coming out.

With the other men, Dan drove his peavey into the twisted mass, wrenching and heaving, searching for the key log which held the jam. The sweat poured down his back and face and ran into his eyes, but looking up the jam only seemed to get higher and higher. Suddenly there came a heave and a great grinding noise, and the top of the jam seemed to hang over him like a projecting eave. He pulled again on the log his peavey held, and the creaking and grinding noises increased as though the jam gathered itself up for some great effort. Then—yes, it was motion. The whole solid wall turned fluid.

"Out from under! Timber!" shouted Dan.

The group of jacks were already pursuing their way shorewards. Frantically Dan turned and leaped from log to log. He heard Spike's warning bark again, but he did not dare to look up. He kept his eyes fixed on the next jump ahead. If a man lost a footing in that mass of tumbling logs nothing but a prayer could save him.

Dan was near shore now. He leaped again, thanking his lucky stars that he had escaped from the middle of that moving wall of destruction. As his feet landed on the slippery log, he felt blinding spasms of pain shoot up his thighs; the log spun and bobbed away from him. He felt himself plunging towards the water; then came a sound of thunder and everything went black.

Later—hours later, years later it seemed—Dan came to. It was dark out, terribly dark. He was dripping wet and cold. He heard the booming of the logs and tried to sit up. He felt a cold tongue slap against his cheek, and he threw his arm up and caught it about Spike's warm, furry neck.

Coming from a great distance away, Dan heard a voice. "Take it easy, Dan, take it easy, boy. You're gonna be all right. Everything's okay."

"Who's that?" Dan asked. He was surprised when his voice only came in a whisper. His mouth felt thick and furred and his throat was dry.

"It's Rusty, Dan," and Dan felt the warm, reassuring hand laid on his shoulder. "Young Doyle got through and Hart's upstream with a gang. He must've stopped that other crew—we're running smooth here. That was a darned nasty crack you got on the head. Lucky you were near shore or they never would have got you."

Dan rubbed his eyes with his knuckles. "Lord, but it's dark, Rusty. What happened to the moon?"

Rusty seemed a long time answering. "Why, the moon's out, Dan. It's as bright as day."

Dan did not question him further. Slowly the truth bore in upon him. He struggled to a sitting position. The hiss and creak of the speeding logs was the only sound to break the silence. Spike nestled close to his side, his nose in Dan's neck, his warmth comforting. It was black—so awfully black. Everything was black, and Dan's head felt as though it would split.

IX

SPIKE LEADS THE WAY

A quiet afternoon silence lay over the town of Swift River. The Swift ran full to its banks, but it had lost the wild, tempestuous uncontrollability of the early spring. Now it swept by with a soft murmur, the only indication of the speed which had given rise to its name being the long ripples along the bank where an occasional boulder pushed up its wet face. An insect shot by, humming, the sun flashing on its underbody so that it looked and sounded like a golden bullet. A bobolink trilled his rollicking call to fun as he flashed across the meadow on the other side of the tracks.

This silence in which small sounds predominated was not a lazy silence. The breeze from the Swift was cool and refreshing despite the heat of the sun, driving men to action.

The jacks were gone. They had felled the forest giants and had ridden their woody steeds, no less wild for being inanimate, into the sawmill ponds. They had collected their pay to spend half of it in some town where a week of riotous living would make up for the months of loneliness in the big sticks. And their going had left Swift River a drowsy, backwater town once more.

Suddenly the silence was broken by a succession of minor sounds from the direction of headquarters, Hart's cabin. Doors slamming, the sound of damp, sticking windows being forced down, and then the rapid pound of a hammer driving nails into soft wood.

Stepping to the porch of his cabin, holding a wash-pan firmly clutched in both hands, Rufe Martin added to the sudden clatter. The water from the pan hit the dirt yard with a solid splat, and Rufe banged the pan on the rail of the porch before hanging it up on a hook outside the door beside the other pans.

Stepping out to the edge of the porch, Rufe shaded his eyes and looked over the small community. He saw Dan Kirk sitting in the sun in front of his cabin with Spike at his side. Rufe raised his hand to wave a friendly greeting, but he checked himself in time. A slow flush crept up his neck, and his hands fell limply to his side. Muttering to himself and shaking his head, he retreated inside the cabin.

Shortly afterwards Rusty Davis, his bowlegged walk resembling a sailor's, came up the dirt path to Dan's cabin. He stopped in front of Dan, his legs widespread. Spike stood up, yawning.

"Hiya, Dan," he said. "How're you feelin'?"

Slowly Dan looked up. He was wearing sun glasses and his skin was pale and drawn. There were hollows in his cheeks, over which the bones stood out like rugged promontories. Here and there on his skin was a patch of black stubble. The hands that rested on his knees were white and the blue veins prominent.

Dan smiled. It was the old smile, but it had a pale quality, refusing to radiate warmth. "Hello, Rusty. I feel pretty good. No headache to-day. I'm saving on aspirin," he replied at last, laughing hollowly.

"You know, Dan," Rusty went on, ignoring the cynicism evident in Dan's tone, "now that everything's pretty well shaken down here we ought to make you a porch. It would keep the sun out of your——" Suddenly realising what he had been about to say, Rusty faltered, embarrassed. His feet shuffled.

"That's all right, Rusty. I don't have to worry about the sun bothering my eyes these days. Besides," he continued, feeling Rusty's embarrassment and making an effort to cheer up, "besides the sun feels good. Warms me clear down to the cockles of me heart, as somebody says—I forget who."

There was a moment's silence, then Rusty spoke up. "Well, mister, come and get it or we'll throw it out."

"Chow time so soon? What's on the menu?"

"Beans again, I guess."

"Beans! Doesn't Rufe know I've been eating beans all winter? I'll be glad when it's time for Jerry to come back, then at least we'll get fish."

Fumbling, Dan's hand found Spike's head, and he grasped both the dog's ears in one hand. "Hear that, boy? Chow time!"

Spike squirmed loose and yawned again. Playfully he took Dan's wrist between his strong teeth and shook his head to and fro.

It was painful to see Dan rise. Clutching the arms of the chair, his knuckles showing white from the strain, he hunched himself up. It was not so much that he was weak as that he was uncertain of all his movements. As he rose, Rusty took him by the arm and guided his faltering steps. Walking down the dirt path, Dan clearly showed the ravages a month's sickness and weeks of mounting despair had wrought on his body. The husky, broad-shouldered chap who had gone into the brush in the fall had been replaced by a stooped, emaciated scarecrow whose clothes hung around him like flapping sails.

Stumbling along in the darkness towards the station, Dan could feel Spike's weight pressing against his legs, reassuring him. Spike had not lost his habit of keeping close to Dan wherever the man went, the habit he had developed since the day Dan went through the ice. He had given up his rollicking, and his days of tramping untrammelled in the woods were only memories now that Dan spent the biggest part of his time sitting in a chair, either inside the cabin or out in the warm sun.

At supper that night Spike lay quietly by Dan's chair, accepting with calm the occasional offerings Dan surreptitiously offered him. At least Dan thought they were surreptitious, but the passage was perfectly obvious to Rufe Martin and Rusty Davis.

The silence that descended upon them now when they ate was not the customary silence of the camps. It was an uneasy silence, more eloquent than words, just as the quiet of the country seems like noise to the city-dweller; and all three rushed pell-mell to fill the empty silence whenever it settled upon them. Rusty and Rufe spoke in great length about the little details of their day, things they thought might amuse Dan; and Dan in turn questioned them minutely because he felt they wanted to be questioned.

But the meals were not as oppressive as they had been when Dan first returned to them. It was less painful now for Rusty and Rufe to watch their friend eat. He had mastered the knack of finding the food on his plate—an elementary thing, yet vital to a person who suddenly finds himself without the aid of sight. But he ate little, pushing back his plate half full, and making up for it by drinking three cups of Rufe's strong coffee.

Afterwards, Dan helped with the dishes. Half leaning, half sitting on the kitchen table, he dried the utensils Rufe passed him. The others insisted that this was unnecessary, but Dan felt less dependent when he could contribute some little work in part payment for his meals.

When the dishes were washed, the three men and the dog trooped over to Dan's cabin. Outside the air was sharp now that the sun had gone down, and they all quickened their pace. Rusty helped Dan light a fire, then they drooped themselves around in attitudes of repose, helping themselves to Dan's tin of tobacco. Rufe sat sprawled across the cot; Rusty leaned in a chair near the table, and Dan sat in a chair by the fire, holding himself stiff and erect. Spike lay at Dan's feet on the rug by the fireplace, his nose almost poked into the roaring flames.

They were all comfortable at last, the smoke drifting in and out of the rafters above their heads like a bellying blue cloud. "Phew!" Rusty said. "This sure is strong tobacco!"

"Noxious weed anyway," Rufe interrupted. "When I was a young 'un we used to call 'em cigar-eets. I can remember us kids gatherin' Sundays down by the hotel—it was general store and post office, too—watchin' the drummers from the East smokin' 'em. To tell you the truth, we was hopin' they'd set their whiskers afire. All the farmers roundabout used to say they was ladies' seegars."

"Rufe," Rusty remarked in a disgusted tone of voice, "you're gettin' the dangdest habit of interruptin' people. How I ever put up with it before's beyond me. Gettin' old, too—always talkin' about when you was a young 'un."

"Now, now, you two love birds," Dan said, laughing—his first real laugh that evening. "This is a fine time to start picking on each other. How many years has it been since——"

"Too darned many," Rufe said, interrupting again. "Besides, he don't even cook."

"You'd get fed up on it too if you had to sling hash for a hundred bear-eatin' animals all day long the whole winter through."

Both men puffed viciously on their pipes and glared at each other. Dan knew there was nothing serious about their bickering; like two people who had lived long together, they loved baiting each other, but both of them had very equable dispositions.

Then the conversation veered to life in the big sticks during the winter. Rufe, having lived all his life on the edge of the industry, was ordinarily very incurious about logging. But the drama of the hidden crew working against Northern seemed to pique his imagination, and now the station-master plied Dan with questions. Besides, both men liked to get Dan to talk as much as possible; then he had less time to brood on his infirmity, and his voice would become animated and a little colour would flash into his cheeks.

Dan retold the story of his going through the ice, of Spike's summoning of the two men, and of his virtual kidnapping by Healy and Read. Afterwards he spoke of the ever-present fear in his mind during their early months in the brush that Spike would one day revert to the wild. He told of the dog's midnight forays and his final decision after the wolf fight to stay with his master.

When Dan had finished his story, there was a moment's silence. Rufe shook his head. "I sure hate to admit it, but I was way off the track as far as that fellow's concerned. He——"

A sharp rap at the cabin door, followed shortly by Jack Hart's white bare head, cut off whatever the gangling station-master was about to say.

"Hello everybody," Hart said. "Am I interrupting an important conference?"

"Heck, no," said Rusty, glancing at Rufe and smiling wickedly. "Just keeping us from one of Rufe's famed observations on nature and man, that's all. I guess we ain't missin' much."

Spike rose from his comfortable position by the fire to sniff the newcomer's leg. Hart reached over and patted the big dog on the head. Recognising him for a friend, Spike suffered himself to be patted, then trotted back to the fire, followed by Hart, who stood in front of the flames warming his fingers. "It feels more like fall than spring," he said, slapping his hands together. "Quite a nip in the air. . . . How do you feel to-day, Dan?"

"Pretty good."

"Any headache?"

Dan shook his head.

"What's Doc Carrol say about it?"

"Same old thing. He said that knock on the head probably shattered the optic nerve, and nothing can be done about that. He said the headaches ought to disappear gradually."

Hart shook his head, a deep frown furrowing his brow. "And the aspirin?" he asked.

"Oh, it was the Doc who recommended I take them," Dan replied.

"Still it doesn't seem right to me," Hart persisted. "Sure you wouldn't like to see a city doctor—a specialist?"

"What's the use? It would only be expensive and what could he tell me—except that I'll be blind for the rest of my life?"

The three men winced. They were tough, they had to be; and sudden death and injury were no strangers to their work. But it hurt them anew every time they saw this young chap whom they had come to like and admire suffer, as he obviously had to suffer, to bring out these words that cut them all to the quick.

It was kind-hearted Rufe who finally came to the rescue. "Just about cleaned up here, Hart?" he asked.

"Just about. I'll be leaving on the work train in the morning. . . . By the way, Dan, I've got a job for you."

"Yes? What is it?"

"Well, we're going to try an experiment next year. We've bought a dozen tractors and a half-dozen trucks. Going to do away with some of the teams. They'll be delivered around the middle of the summer, and I want Rusty here to put 'em under cover."

"Whoa, just a second," Rusty said. "Horses, yes, but I ain't never handled one of them pesky contraptions at——"

"Don't interrupt, and pay attention," Rufe said, grinning. "Dan'll furnish the brains, all you have to worry about is the brawn. Right, Mr. Hart?"

N

"Essentially," said the smiling Hart. "Dan can show you how to run them and you can put them in the barn where we keep the old skids. We're going to send a crew up six weeks earlier this year, to put the road to Camp One in good shape. . . . Think you can handle that, Dan?"

"I guess I haven't forgotten," Dan replied somberly.

"Good!"

Nothing was said for a moment as the smoke from Hart's pipe rose and joined that already floating in and out of the rafters. Then: "What's new, Mr. Hart—about Healy and his gang, I mean?" It was Kirk who spoke.

Hart looked up quickly. The frown had disappeared only to return again. "Nothing new, Dan," he replied thoughtfully. "They're still in jail. But I'm beginning to think you were right. I hear rumours that money will be available to spring them in another month. Already the trial's been pushed way down the court calendar, and once they're sprung —Healy, McQuade, Read and the rest—it'll probably be pushed down indefinitely."

"What are we going to do about it?" Dan demanded truculently, his cheeks flushed.

"What can we do? You know what happened to your Dad's company. We'll certainly never collect damages because we can't prove the tie-up with Great Western. And I'm beginning to think we'll be lucky to get satisfaction from the gang who did the job. You can't buck power without power. At any rate a company worth thousands can't do real damage to

one worth millions. We've just got to keep our
fingers crossed and be glad—thanks to you—that we
got our timber to market this year. We'll certainly
keep a weather eye peeled next year."

Hart hated to talk in this vein. He knew, or suspected, that one thing keeping Dan going was his
hope for a conviction against Great Western. Right
now revenge was of more value to him then any
loving care, but Hart could not keep on pretending
that they would get the conviction when he was
almost certain that, on the contrary, they would not.

"By the way, Mr. Hart, whatever happened that
night?" Rufe wanted to know. "Rusty here's so
mum I think there must be an owl amongst his
ancestors."

"Pay no attention, Mr. Hart. He just wants to
hear the gory details."

Hart smiled wanly. "Well, Rufe," he said, "it was
really very simple. None of us knew anything was
wrong beforehand. Of course I had wondered what
was keeping Dan so long, but I figured he wanted to
complete the cruising before he came into camp.
What neither of us knew was that while we were
dickering over buying that property it was practically sold to Great Western, and in the summer they
evidently put a crew in there to fell the timber for
the drive. That property's not worth a confederate
nickel unless they have us sewed up lock, stock and
barrel, for otherwise they haven't any way to get
the logs out. By starting that jam they figured on
being able to prevent us from getting to market in
time. Then they would make an offer that we

couldn't refuse, and, presto, both properties would be theirs.

"At any rate, we were two or three miles upriver from Camp Three, everything looked much as usual and I was posting the men when young Doyle socked me on the shoulder. He was wheezing and puffing like an old horse with asthma. Dan had been suspicious of Great Western all along, and I guess made me quite wary, too, so I knew there wasn't a minute to lose. We called in the boys who had been posted downstream and went off up the Swift at a dogtrot. We were clean out of puff and I was beginning to think Dan had been a little too premature when we heard it—the boom of another drive coming down that cut-off from the Cranmer River.

"Well, I've broken up many a jam in my life, but it was the first time I was ever called upon to start one. But we knew if that drive ever hit the Swift it was curtains. Lucky for me that was a good gang of bushwhackers. In less time than it takes to tell, they jumped in, tossing logs over their shoulders, building them up in small piles starting from the shore, twisting logs up endwise and throwing them together like so many matchsticks—that before long we had a pretty respectable jam in that cut-off and the Swift was running clear. By that time, as you know, Dan had the jam by the junction broken and we were out of the woods. That's all there was to it."

"What about that other outfit?" asked Rufe.

"Oh, them! Well, by that time the boys were a little tired and just a wee bit riled. Some of Healy's gang made the mistake of coming down to see what was causing the stoppage and if their drive had hit the Swift properly. By the time our lads got through with 'em there was a broken leg or two and a couple of hospital cases. Not one of them got away, although we caught Healy trying to launch a canoe in the Cranmer, the blamed fool. Might have been better if we'd let him go. Then he'd have drowned and we'd have been rid of one more rat."

"McQuade and his cronies didn't try to make a break," Rusty offered. "They was scared stiff. If what you say about the bail business is true, it might have been better if we'd given 'em a good lacin'."

"What's this I heard about trouble between One and Two?" Dan asked.

"Nobody found out for sure, but evidently they were trying to pull the same stunt there—Great Western, I mean. But the situation wasn't as good so they gave it up after tipping a few of the big fellows—forty footers—in. Never did catch any of them. Well, Rufe, that answer your question?"

Rufe nodded. "Just about," he said.

After that the four men talked about more immediate things, about the tractors and the possibility of running good roads up as far as Camp Four. In a half-hour or so, Rusty Davis caught himself yawning. "That settles it," he said. "It's way past my bed time."

"Me too," Rufe said, rising. "Work train leaves in the morning. Better get down and get my year's work done."

Spike got up with them, giving a delicious long stretch, legs wide-spread, quivering; then he yawned and followed the two to the door.

"Good-night, Dan. Pleasant dreams."

"So long," Dan answered.

Hart remained seated. "I'll be with you in a little while, Rusty," he said. "I want to talk to Dan a minute." Rusty nodded, and buttoning up his coat disappeared into the night.

Hart threw another log on the dying embers. "You know you saved my neck up there, don't you, Dan?"

"Forget it. Anybody else would have done the same."

"Maybe. The fact remains that you were on the spot and you did the right thing. You not only saved my neck but you saved Northern's life. If that drive hadn't got to the sawmill. . . . Well, a whole lot of us would've been out looking for a job."

Hart looked dreamily at the fire for a minute, then: "Now I'm going to tell you something and I don't want you to get huffy about it. Promise?"

"Anything within reason, Mr. Hart."

"Not 'mister'—Jack. And this has to be a definite promise."

"Okay . . . Jack. I promise."

"Good. Well, then, here it is. In consideration of your services to the company, we—that is, Northern Lumber—are offering you a pension. Now, just a minute—don't get all hepped up. It won't be a fortune, but it'll be enough so that you can live comfortably for the rest of your days. And another thing. Don't think they're giving you this out of gratitude. It's just hard-headed business to reward anyone who's been clever enough to get the company out of a jam. Now think it over, and don't say no."

Hart nervously watched Dan's face. The man's muscles had tightened until his cheekbones were more prominent then ever. His mouth twitched and there was a suspicion of moistness rolling from beneath the dark glasses.

"Let's—give me a cigarette," Dan muttered brokenly.

Suddenly, wearily, "Okay, Jack, I'll take it. I can't live forever on the kindness of Rufe and Rusty."

Hart grinned. "You don't have to act enthusiastic if you don't want to. I know it goes against the grain, but so do a lot of other things a whole lot less pleasant to take. Have you made any plans?"

"Plans?"

"Yes. Have you decided what you're going to do with yourself?"

"Learn Braille to start with, I guess," Dan said bitterly.

For just a moment Hart sought for a suitable answer. "You know, Dan," he began quietly, "Jim Kirk never was a quitter. And I don't think his son is either, although right now he needs a good swift kick in the pants. You're not licked, man! Think what this pension means, for instance. Men fight years for a little steady income like that. Why? Because it means freedom. Perfect freedom. You can

do what you like. Of course, you can't sit back and
expect to get wealthy. But it relieves you of the
constant little bickering, griping worries . . ."
Hart rose to his feet, "I'll be back in a month or so,
Dan, and I want a more intelligent answer because
I'm going to ask you that question again." Hart
slipped on his jacket and moved to the door. "Don't
think I'm trying to lord it over you. I knew Jim
Kirk and liked him. I'm only telling you what he
would have told you. . . . So long, now."

Dan's hesitation was barely noticeable. "So long,
Jack. Thanks for everything."

"Don't thank me—thank yourself. And remember: I'll be waiting for that answer. Good-night,
Dan." Hart pronounced the last sentence like a
benediction and went out into the night.

"I don't like it," Hart said. He was sitting on the
edge of the bunk removing his shoes and socks.
Rusty was already in bed, just the tip of his nose
showing outside the blankets.

"You don't like what?" he asked.

"The way Dan's acting."

"Me either."

"Why, even the dog is listless and uninterested. I
wish there was some way we could snap him out of
it. If he could only get off on his own, do something,
break away from those thoughts of his, get out of
that chair and that cabin . . ." The sentence trailed
away as Hart stopped in the middle of his undressing
and stared at the floor, trying to see a way out.

"You know," Rusty said, sitting up in bed and

letting the blankets fall to his waist, "I've been thinking. Durin' the war I had a buddy who got hit with a piece of sharpnel, and he lost his sight. Well, after the war they sent him into Switzerland for his health, and when he comes back he has a dog with him. I wish you'd seen the guy. You'd never know he was blind. That dog led him anywhere he wanted to go, and darned if he didn't go a blamed sight faster than when he had his own eyes. Well, that first dog died and that fellow almost didn't get over it. But he sent away for another one and now he runs a farm in Iowa."

"There's a place back East that furnishes dogs like that now," Hart said, scratching his head. "What was your idea—to get one for Dan?"

"Heck, no! Dan's got one. All we need to do is train him."

"Spike?"

Rusty nodded.

"Well, I don't know . . ." Hart began.

"Why not?" Rusty asserted. "He's a Shepherd— the kind they use. He's smart enough. And the biggest problem after they get through trainin' 'em is how the man and his new pal are goin' to get along. We don't have to worry about that. That dog's sun sets and rises in Dan. And look how Spike feels responsible for him. He tags Dan around like a shadow. I think it'd be simple."

"Maybe. It's worth a try, at least. Why don't you talk to Dan about it in the morning?"

"I will," Rusty said. He pulled the blankets over his head again and in a minute he was snoring.

Dan Kirk lay on his back in the cot, the blankets pushed down to his feet. It was still warm in the cabin, and he was too restless to sleep. With his left hand he gently fingered Spike's soft fur, where the dog lay asleep by his bed. Evidently he awakened the dog, for he felt a soft, moist tongue lick his wrist. He felt that that reassuring moist touch was the only thing keeping him sane in a maddening world.

What were his plans, Hart had asked. Well, what were they? What could they be? He saw no choice facing him. A growing thickness lumped in his throat so that he had difficulty swallowing, the anger throbbed in his temples, and he had a splitting headache. It would not have been so bad had his efforts been of some use, but it was apparent that McQuade and Healy and the rest would escape the slippery hands of justice. It was bad enough that Great Western had got off scot free. And now . . .!

When they first told him he would be blind, heaven knows that had been a bleak day! But the strength of his misery had been balanced by the unreasonableness of his hope. Now he had lost hope, and the despair, though no more pressing than it had been at first, was almost too much to bear.

A year ago he had been in despair, too. Yes, but that was different. He had his sight then, a strong body; he had his knowledge and could put it to good use. Now his knowledge was no good to him. He was of no use to anyone—except as a drag on their efforts. Bleakly, Dan turned his face to the wall and pounded the rough logs with his bare fist. The pain relieved him. He turned his face into the pillow and after a few minutes passed into a deep but troubled slumber.

The next morning dawned clear, but the summery feeling of the day before had vanished as a cold, bitter wind blew through the small settlement. After they had seen the chugging work-train puff its way up the tracks, carrying with it the last vestiges of the winter logging operations, the three men and the dog repaired to the station-master's cabin for breakfast.

It was during breakfast that Rusty Davis, with many an anxious glance at Dan, broached his plan for the training of Spike as a guide. Rufe, who had not before heard of the plan, was at once chatteringly enthusiastic. Kirk, however, was non-committal. It was not until Rusty started talking about his friend's farm in Iowa and how he succeeded in running it and getting around everywhere with the aid of his dog that Dan began to show interest. Seeing that Dan was interested—there was colour in his cheeks and he straightened up in his chair—Rusty immediately continued with his story.

"Gus—that's my buddy's name, Gus," Rusty explained, "used to like to sit out on his porch every evenin' while the rest of the boys were finishin' up the chores. Well, down the road a bit lived a nice old widow, and this widow sort of kept a weather eye peeled on Gus. After all he had a pretty decent farm and he was supposed to have a lot of silver in his overalls. Long about sundown that widow used to get in her buggy, ride down the road, and then turn into the lane to ask about Gus's health. Well, somehow Gus always managed to hear the widow comin'—there was either a field hand there to tell him or he'd hear the tyres on the gravel. Gus kept a silk bandanna handy and he'd whip this out and make believe to be asleep, and the widow'd tiptoe up, and look at him, sayin', 'Tsk, tsk, poor man!' and go away again.

"Well, this particular night I'm talkin' about Gus must've been dozin' off anyway, because he didn't hear the widow's buggy come up the lane. A field hand comes runnin' up, but he's too late—the widow gets down and buttonholes Gus and starts chatterin' and all the field hand could do was stand there and grin. Well, Lady—that's Gus's dog—couldn't make head or tail of the whole business. She cocks her head first on one side, then on the other, and first she looks at Gus and then she looks at the widow. All of a sudden Lady jumps up and runs into the house, and in a minute she comes out and what do you think she has? Yes, sir, that dog had a silk bandanna in her mouth. She put her feet up on Gus's chair and tried to put that handkerchief into his lap. By that time the field hand was in stitches. Gus asks him what's the matter, cranky like, and when he finds out he laughs and roars and pounds his knees till he gets blue in the face and his eyes pop. And the widow—she gets up in the huff, hitches up the buggy, and never comes back!"

When the laughter had died down—Dan had really

laughed so hard that the tears ran down his face—
Rusty said, "Well, Dan, how about it?"

"You win," Dan replied. "When do we start?"

"Whoa, now, wait just a minute," Rusty hastily
asserted. "This ain't done overnight, you know."

"How long's it take to train one of them dogs?"
Rufe inquired.

"Four to six months, for an ordinary dog." Rusty
answered so promptly that Dan suspected he had
given the matter a great deal of thought if he had
not been reading up on training dogs. As a matter
of fact, Rusty's limited knowledge was pieced out
with long detailed letters from Hart and various
magazine articles and books Hart sent throughout
the summer. "Of course," Rusty added, smiling,
"Spike ain't an ordinary dog. Still it might take
even him a month."

"When do we start?" Dan persisted.

Rusty scratched his head. His sales talk had been
a little too successful for his own good, for he had
intended to start inventory this day.

"How about first thing after lunch?" he suggested.

Dan nodded. "It's a date." For the first time since
the accident Dan had something to look forward to
—something that didn't carry with it a presentiment
of fear. After the dishes were washed, he said to the
station-master, "Mind if I stick around, Rufe?"

Martin raised a quizzical eyebrow and stared
steadily at Kirk for a full minute. Hitherto Dan
had always returned to his own cabin, much to the
station-master's chagrin.

"Gosh, no, Dan," he replied. "Glad to have you.

I haven't had a good gab in a long time. Rusty ain't
fit company at all any more—I'm gettin' so I have
to talk to myself."

"What do you want me to do?"

"Just sit and talk—or you can peel those spuds if
you want."

"Do you trust me?"

Rufe laughed. This was more like the old Dan;
he was all right if he could laugh at himself. "No,
not exactly," he replied, "but I got me one of them
newfangled parin' knives this winter. You can do
your darndest and still she won't take off anything
but peel."

So Dan sat and peeled potatoes and talked to Rufe.
And when Rufe was out of the room he talked to
the dog, speaking to him in great detail about his
new duties and how soon Dan expected him to learn
them. Spike lay at Dan's feet or sat on his haunches
looking at the man, and whenever Dan became too
talkative the dog growled and chewed at Dan's foot,
as if to say: "You can't scare me. As long as I'm
with you, what's a little work? When do we start?"

At long last the afternoon came—the afternoon,
that was to start the dog learning a new skill, teaching him yet another way to serve the master he
loved ; and an afternoon that would end, after many
weeks, in taking the shuffle out of Dan's feet, bringing the slow, groping hands down to his sides,
sending his head up, his shoulders back.

Rusty returned with a short length of leather that
he had fashioned into a leash for Spike. The dog
had never been trained to a leash before, Dan having

had no difficulty in instructing the dog to obey commands without it. But it was necessary if Dan was to be led properly that he knew what Spike was doing, and so the leash was a necessary evil.

When the strap was snapped to his collar, Spike looked over his shoulder with a puzzled expression to see what all the fuss was about; but outside of taking the leash in his mouth once or twice, he gave the men little trouble. In a week or so he had become so accustomed to it that he would run and fetch the leash to Dan whenever it was time for his training period. Spike seemed to regard these training periods, coming at regular intervals every day, an hour in the morning and an hour in the afternoon, more as an outing specially prepared for him—like the old runs he and Dan used to have in the woods—than actual work.

They started in very gradually at first, Dan letting himself be led and giving commands and Rusty furnishing the sight. Spike was already well trained in obedience, but a week was spent nevertheless in putting the dog through his paces in order to get him used to the feel of the leash. Three or four new commands were added to those he already knew—"forward," "right," "left," "up"—the last being the command Dan used in climbing stairs. At the end of the week, Spike would stop or turn on a penny and sit patiently, motionless, until Dan gave him the word to move forward. As he had done before, so now Dan relied on voice and intonation for getting his wishes across clearly to the dog. Rusty, feeling that the dog should recognise but one master, refrained as much as possible from rebuking Spike. Praise was bestowed by a word—"well done," "good dog," "attaboy"—or by a pat on the head. When Spike responded incorrectly, he was reprimanded not by a blow but by a reproachful word. His two trainers began by using the reproachful words "bad" or "drummer," but gradually the expression "phooey" came into greater favour. Rusty or Dan only had to say, "Phooey, Spike," putting into the word all the disdain they felt, for the dog, his ears flattened, his tail carried between his legs, to look guiltily up at them from underneath lowered brows.

The next step consisted in teaching the dog the path from Dan's cabin to the station-master's cabin, where now Dan ate all his meals. Rusty had his doubts about this procedure, but Dan reasoned it out for him. "It's like this," he explained. "You're right in the sense that if we teach him to do some things by memory, he'll depend on memory for everything, instead of thinking out things for himself. But meanwhile I've got to go back and forth, and as long as he's learning other things in his training, and as long as I don't work him by himself over any different terrain, I don't think it'll hurt any."

The way to Martin's cabin was just a narrow dusty path worn by countless footsteps. It took two or three twists and turns to avoid big rocks and there were two or three spots where the path dipped suddenly. To a person with sight there was nothing particularly difficult about the path, even at night, but to a blind person the path offered a dozen hidden pitfalls. The problem was to stay in the centre of the rut, else a sudden step in either direction might result in a twisted ankle.

Inside of ten days Spike had learned the path by heart, cautiously leading Dan around the turns, pressing against him to warn of the sudden declivities, and tugging hard at the leash when he wanted the man to follow straight behind him in the centre of the path. But what is more important, this first major job gave the dog an inkling of what was expected of him in the future. It was a study to see the dog's expression the first time he brought Dan over the path alone. He sat by Dan's chair, proudly looking first at Rusty then at Rufe as though to say, "Well, I got him here, didn't I? And by myself too." Just as a child learning the piano will get an extra incentive out of his practice if he is allowed to play a simple piece like "America," so did this independent responsibility stimulate Spike's eagerness in his training periods.

Stairs did not prove to be as big a stumbling-block as the men had anticipated. Since the day Dan went through the ice, Spike's habit had been to walk close beside the man instead of running ahead —except for steps or stairs, when he would dash up them four at a time and sit at the top awaiting Dan's tortuously slow climb. Patiently they made it clear to the dog that Dan could not run up steps as blithely as he could, and he soon learned to give adequate warning and to climb slowly, making sure Dan's feet were planted securely before going on. This was a skill he could practice alone with Dan; it was not long before he was as letter perfect in this as he was about the path.

Then, at last, came the dog's serious training. Hour after hour, morning after morning, week after week, never losing their tempers, the two men worked with the dog, giving the dog one problem in the morning and helping him solve it, letting him work out the same problem unaided in the afternoon over different ground.

It was during one of these morning workouts that they discovered how inadequately the leash transferred the dog's reactions to Dan. To teach Spike the abstract principle of avoiding any obstacle Dan might encounter, Rusty had constructed a maze of a dozen boxes of different heights scattered irregularly over the ground. It was Spike's task to lead Dan in and out of the boxes towards Rusty, who was stationed at the opposite end, without letting the man stumble. The first two or three times Spike tackled the problem, he led Dan carefully around the boxes at the beginning of the maze only to become bored and lead the man directly towards Rusty. After a few days he got the point, however, and twisted and turned through the maze without an error. This was fine until Rusty moved the boxes closer together. Then, no matter how well the dog turned, Dan inevitably stumbled against the corners of the boxes, unable to feel Spike's movements quickly enough. This was not so good. Rusty scratched his head and mumbled, and they decided to call it quits for the day.

After lunch that noon Rusty disappeared. Returning at suppertime, he dropped a curious leather contraption at Dan's feet. "What do you think of that, Dan?" he asked. It was apparently a harness of some sort, Dan decided, with two loosely joined straps and a rigid hoop, like the handle of a baby carriage, fastened to the straps.

"What's this for? Spike?"

"Yep," Rusty replied. "Saw a picture of it somewheres. You see, that leash was okay, but it was too loose—the dog had to knock you in the legs for you to get what he was doin'. This way these straps fasten around his belly and chest and you grab the handle, then no matter how he moves you feel it."

Rusty was right. Dan tried the new harness the next morning, and if Spike had been a help to him before, now it was like having his eyesight back. Not a movement of Spike's nervous body escaped being transmitted through the harness to Dan's inquisitive fingers.

"How's she work?" Rusty inquired, after Kirk had gone through the maze a half a dozen times without a hitch.

"Works swell," said Dan, grinning with excitement and happiness. "I can almost feel what he's thinking."

Both Rusty and Dan were amazed at the progress Spike made. It was only natural, though, that Spike should have the advantages over a young, untrained dog. First of all he was older, accustomed to obeying Dan without question. And the love he bore his master made him anxious to serve the man in any way he could.

"I never saw anything like it, Dan," Rusty said one day. "Why, I bet if you told him to jump in front of a train he'd do it. You should see the look in his eyes when he watches you."

"I don't have to see it, Rusty," Dan replied. "I can feel it whenever he's around."

But the greatest reason for the dog's rapid progress was the sense of responsibility he felt towards Kirk. That sense had been with him, almost from the first, but the training developed it to a point where Spike had no hesitation in disobeying Dan's commands if he knew these commands were wrong.

It was the point of certain exercises he was put through to develop this sense. For instance, in judging heights. Two boxes were placed on the ground four feet apart and a light plank stretched across them at a height that would just permit Spike to walk under it. The dog walked under the plank safely but Dan barked his shins. Gradually the plank was raised till Dan could clear it, and by that time Spike had become a pretty accurate judge of Dan's height. Such exercises not only served to develop a particular skill—estimating heights in this case—but it also led the dog to the inescapable general conclusion that there were many things which he as a dog could do and which Dan as a human being could not. Once the dog had learned this, active disobedience when Dan's safety was at stake became a part of his sense of responsibility.

And so the summer months came and lengthened

into days of blistering heat. Dan put on weight; his cheeks filled out and took on colour; his walk was no longer slow and stumbling; and his hands had lost their scrawny appearance and their death-like pallor. Now he was too tired out at night from healthy exercise to lie awake pitying himself and bemoaning his fate. Fearful of reawakening his moody despondency, the two older men held back for some time the news that McQuade and Healy and their gang had been released on bail; but the announcement had no visible effect on Dan. Busily fitting the pieces of a plan together like a jigsaw in the back of his mind, Dan refused to worry about minor details. The day would come for dealing with Great Western, but that day had not arrived as yet. First he must learn to overcome his handicap by teaching Spike to be his eyes.

In the middle of the summer the trucks and trac-tors were delivered, and several days of Spike's training lapsed while Dan taught Rusty how to drive them. Later they spent two weeks driving carefully over the rough road to Camp One, marking the weak parts of the road and the places where it would have to be widened with stakes and red flags so that when the road gang came up everything would be ready for them. Luckily Dan could not see the mistakes Rusty made or he would have worn out the floor boards frantically hunting for the brakes on his side of the truck, for the bewildered little man was a very sketchy driver. Spike had no qualms, however, clamouring eagerly for a ride whenever they went out. He had discovered a new pleasure—the ecstasy of sitting beside his master on the front seat of the truck and leaning out.

One evening nearly four months from the day Spike's training began, the three men sat on Martin's porch, enjoying the refreshing night air. Now that Dan was himself once more, they had resumed their old habit of silence, and they would sit for many minutes without a word, finding entertainment in just companionship.

From where he sat leaning tipped back against the wall of the cabin, Dan could hear the familiar thud of Rusty's knife stabbing into the much-marked floor boards. Then the sound ceased and Rusty spoke.

"Well, Dan, shall we give him the works to-morrow?"

Dan leaned forward, letting his chair come down with a bump. "Okay, Rusty," he replied. "If he's not ready now, he never will be."

The "he" was Spike. It had been agreed between the two men at the start of his training to give the dog a final examination when both of them felt he was ready for it. If he passed the test, well and good; his training was completed. If he failed disastrously there was nothing they could do but own up that the whole business had been a sorry mistake.

The following morning after breakfast the three men and the dog assembled in front of Martin's cabin. It was cloudy and cool, nevertheless Dan felt beads of sweat on his forehead and his hands were wet and clammy. Even Spike seemed to realise something was afoot. Instead of sitting still, he

nervously stood then sat again, and finally he grasped
Dan's ankle in his jaws to reassure himself that
everything was all right. Davis had marked out a
difficult course for the dog to follow, one that wan-
dered from the cabin across the train embankment,
over the feeder, back again, down through the
centre of the settlement, off to the river, through a
patch of wild, clinging brush, and then back to
Martin's cabin. It was over three miles long. Rusty
would follow as judge and to explain to Dan where
to go, and Rufe, his yellow hair straggling in every
direction, would go along as a spectator.

"All set?" Rusty asked.

"All set," Dan replied through clenched teeth.
"Forward, Spike!"

Spike set out at a quick moving pace down to the
railroad embankment, leading Dan up the loose
cinder bed and across the rails without mishap. He
herded Dan across the narrow plank that served as a
bridge, then kept him on the top of the feeder bank
where the going was easier for the man. They recrossed the feeder a hundred yards down the track
by another plank bridge. Watching, Rufe Martin,
who had not seen Spike in action before, held his
breath as the dog seemed to send Dan running across
the plank. But as neither Dan stumbled nor fell,
his heart came back in place again.

It was when they were in the centre of the settlement trotting over the wooden sidewalks that Spike
really showed his mettle. Purposely Rusty sent
Dan around one block twice. The first time there
was nothing out of the ordinary to bother the dog,

but as they passed a spot where the sidewalk crossed a trifling gulley like a bridge, Rusty tore up three of the loose boards and put them to one side. The sidewalk was about a foot off the ground, but at this particular place it was closer to two feet, and an unsuspecting tumble into this open space could give Dan a bad shaking up.

They trotted around the block again, and this time they came to the gaping blank in the middle of the sidewalk. Puzzled, Spike hesitated for just a moment. The space was easy enough for him to jump, but he was more confused from the fact that the hole should not have been there. Dan, not re-alising what Rusty had done, shook the harness impatiently and whispered, "Forward, Spike." When the dog still did not move, Dan hissed out the cor-recting expression "phooey."

Gently, as though he were handling a baby, Spike put his body between Dan and the gaping hole, pressed Dan backwards a few yards, hesitated to show Dan the step, then led him off the sidewalk into the road and back on the sidewalk again ten feet past the gap. Rusty sighed and grinned happily. Rufe, a suspicion of wet film covering his eyes, looked at Rusty and nodded vigorously. To the gangling station-master this action of Spike's was nothing less than a miracle.

Spike covered the rest of the course without a hitch. On through town, then up the slippery grassy approach to a barn where teams were sheltered during the logging season, down the back stairs that were minus a rail, with a drop of fifteen feet from the top step to the concrete floor of the stable. On down the narrow river path, skirting boulders and the more troublesome loose stones. Around vines and low-hanging trees, in and out of the brush to the north, and finally back the dirt road to Martin's cabin.

It was nearly noon by the time they got back, and the sun lurked behind the dirty blue clouds, cutting off any air and leaving the atmosphere damp and sticky. The men sat on the steps of the porch, dripping wet and grinning like fools. Over and over again they discussed Spike's merits, his uncanny wisdom, his love for Dan, his sense of responsibility, comparing him with all the dogs of fact and fiction they had ever heard of. Spike sat on his haunches, dripping tongue lolling out, watching and laughing at them with an amused expression, unconcerned by all the talk. But he knew he had done well when he found in his food tin that noon the chopped-up remains of Martin's best steak.

That evening after supper, just as Dan and the two older men were about to troop out to the porch for their siesta, the chattering telegraph in Martin's office clattered out a request from Hart to send Jerry up a month sooner than usual. That was all that was needed to end the holiday feeling of the day on a satisfying note.

Shuddering, the balking engine overshot the little station and came to a stop several hundred feet below. "He was goin' so good he hated to shut her off," Martin commented, blaming the engineer.

The men ran down the tracks, but before they could get to the train a laughing figure in a light summer dress swung loosely away from the steps and reached up to receive the packages the conductor handed down to her. In another minute she was enveloped by three husky men and a huge, barking tan dog.

"Here, stand away, let's get a good look at you," Dan said at last, the greetings having been repeated half a dozen times and the train having snorted indignantly away.

For a moment the two older men were abashed at the straight young girl standing before them. The slim, boyish girl they had sent away in the fall had been replaced by one not so slim, much taller and, alas, no longer boyish.

Shyly Jerry stood in front of Dan. He reached out and put his hands on her shoulders and felt the long flaxen hair that she had not yet cut. She was a good head taller than she had been last fall, and the top of her head came up to Dan's shoulders. Running his hands lightly over her face, Dan suddenly drew his hand away. A frown furrowed his forehead, and pretending to be angry, he held up a finger smudged with red lipstick and said, "Here, young lady, what's this?"

It was a pity Dan could not see the blush that reached the roots of her hair. "Never mind, that's only finishing school make-up. It'll come off when I find my overalls. Besides, I'm fourteen now if you please."

Laughing, the men picked up Jerry's suitcase and hustled her off to breakfast.

"Be careful of those two black ones, Uncle Dave," she called out. "They're a surprise for Dan."

Her mouth full of food, Jerry mumbled later, "H'm, boy, is this good. You don't get food like this at school."

They sat around the breakfast table talking until it was time for lunch. After the dishes were washed Rusty sneaked away, and from across the clearing in the direction of Dan's cabin came the mysterious sound of pounding. Dan wanted to go to see what Davis was doing, but Jerry imperiously commanded him to sit down.

"That's part of the surprise," she said. "Now tell me everything about Spike. When are you going to let me watch him work?"

Dan laughed. "Don't let him hear you talk that way. He'll be more conceited than ever. He thinks it's play." Then Dan explained about the dog's training, how quickly he had learned, and how proud they were of him. Afterwards they took a walk along the river, Spike prancingly showing off his accomplishments as Jerry, looking boyish again now that she had put on overalls, followed them around oh-ing and ah-ing at everything.

The afternoon seemed to pass on golden wings, and that evening as the men and the girl and the dog were gathered in Dan's cabin, they felt as a group more contentment than they had known in a year.

"Now, everybody settled?" Jerry asked. The men nodded, "Be quiet, every one," she commanded.

They were so quiet you could hear the rush of the Swift in the distance. Then a scratching sound pulsated through the cabin—just like a phonograph, Dan thought. Spike, sitting between Dan's legs, cocked his head first to one side then on the other at the noise. The scratching sound ceased, and a deep resonant voice filled the small cabin: " *The Black Tulip*, by Alexandre Dumas, a talking book recorded solely for the use of blind. 'Chapter One. On the twenty-first of August, 1662 . . .'" Slowly, distinctly, the voice read on, pouring into the small room the magic words of the great French story-teller. Silently, enchanted, the men sat and listened.

When Jerry shut off the record at the end of the first chapter, no one said a word. "Well, Dan, how did you like it?" Jerry asked.

"Swell!" he replied. "Let's have more."

"Not to-night. It's a small book, and if you hear it all now you won't have anything for the rest of the week."

"Okay," Dan laughed. "Going to ration me, eh?"

Finally Rufe found his voice. Scratching his mop of yellow hair, he said, "Well, I never was a great hand at readin', but this beats all. I could listen to that all night long."

"You could but you ain't goin' to," Rusty said truculently. "You heard what Jerry said—make it last."

"Where did you get it?" Dan asked.

"Dad got it for you—from the library in Washington. They're free, and you can have another one when you've finished this."

And so the pattern of their days were set until the road gang came to Swift River. In the morning Dan helped Rusty with his chores, keeping the camp gear in shape. After lunch he and the dog took long walks through the woods with Jerry or sat and fished. And two or three nights a week the small community gathered in Dan's cabin to hear the magic words of the talking books.

Leading a full, contented life, Dan recovered some of the calm he had found in this group of friends before. Gradually the first stunning shock of his blindness wore off. With Spike to lead him, he was dependent on no one, and with the small monthly pension Hart had arranged for him he had no worries about money for food and tobacco and clothing. In his growing contentment he forgot to regard himself as an incomplete man, and what is more, he forgot the burning desire for revenge that had first brought him to Swift River, and the fact that Great Western and J. P. Schwartz had still not paid for their crimes against him and his father and Northern Lumber.

That is he had almost forgotten, until one day a telegram from Hart brought all the memory back, the recollection that he was still not whole and the recollection that he still had a debt to pay Great Western. He and Jerry had just started out on one of their tramps when Rufe Martin brought them back with a shout. He read the telegram to Dan. "Have arranged consultation with Dr. Howard, Chicago. Have explained your case. It is possible operation might be successful. Wire reply."

In these few words all Dan's contentment fled.
He had been living in a fool's paradise.

"You goin', Dan?" Martin asked.

Dan nodded.

He left on the first stage of the journey to Chicago
on the train that brought the road gang into Swift
River. As Dan was about to board the train, a sym-
pathetic logger reached over to help him up the
steps, but Spike swiftly drew Dan out of the way
of the outstretched arm, waited till Dan had found
the bottom step, then leaped up beside him, waving
his bushy brown tail in the direction of the only
town the dog had known.

X

PAID OFF

WITH the increased sensitiveness that had come to
him since he lost his sight, Dan could almost feel
the muffled breathing of the white-gowned spectators as they sat on the edge of galleried seats in
the small, domed, immaculate operating room. He
could not see the carved, many-paned windows on
the opposite side of the room. It would have helped
if he could. He could have counted the panes. He
tried not to think of the breathing as it seemed to
grow in intensity, almost as if the spectators had
come down from their seats and were sitting closely
huddled around him. He thought instead of the

soft feel of Spike's head as he patted him before they wheeled him into the operating room and shut the dog out.

Suddenly he felt a hand press against his shoulder, the fingers pinched his flesh. "Hello, Kirk. How do you feel? This must seem like pie to an old lumberjack like yourself. Don't worry, we'll have you out of it in a jiffy." Dr. Howard's voice faded and Dan heard the soft padding of the doctor's rubber-soled shoes as he walked away.

To quiet his pounding heart, Dan tried to think of the exact words Dr. Howard had spoken the other day. This was a trick he had learned from his father long ago, the effort at memory having a remarkable effect on slowing down the heart beat. Hitherto he had always recited poetry—"By the shores of Gitchee Gumee," since that was the only poem he could recall exactly. Now he tried to fix Dr. Howard's words in his memory.

"Shattered optic nerve?" Dr. Howard had begun. "Nonsense! You've got some kind of pressure on the nerve tract, true—that's what gives you the headaches. But the nerves are all right. It's like water coming from a hose. Step on the hose and what happens? The water refuses to come out. Pressure on the nerve and the sight impulses refuse to come through. What we're going to do is to take the foot off the hose."

Recalling now the doctor's words, Dan wished fervently with all his heart that the doctor was correct in his diagnosis. Before he had time to do any more thinking, he heard a strange voice.

"Ever had ether before?" the voice asked.

Dan shook his head—as well as he was able. They had shaved the hair from the back of his head and now he noticed for the first time how strange it felt.

"There's nothing to it," the voice continued. "When I give the word, breathe into this. Take long, deep breaths. Just let yourself go and it'll be okay. All right now, you can start breathing."

Dan felt the cup-shaped thing being pressed to his mouth. It fitted over his nose and mouth, and it smelled of rubber. He took a very deep breath and trembled as the sickeningly sweet air made him gasp.

"That's right. Breathe deeper."

He breathed again, trying hard not to fill his lungs so deeply this time, but somehow his lungs were full, and almost immediately he felt himself slipping. He could see now: he was sitting on a yellow, daffodil-kissed cloud and in his ear was the faraway voice like some one mumbling in his sleep or like the sound of rumbling, soft tumbling, far, far distant surf. "That's right, breathe deeply. Take a deep breath. Deep . . . breath . . . take . . . breath . . . breath . . ." And he knew no more.

Several days later Dan was sitting up in bed, his arms clasped tightly to his sides to keep them from trembling, his palms damp with sweat.

Dr. Howard said, "Don't worry, Kirk. We'll soon have you out of suspense."

Dan laughed nervously, and in his nervousness became talkative. "Oh, I'm not worried—or nervous either, Doctor. I feel sure you've done the trick." But his knees shook and he had to wipe his wet hands on the coverlet of the bed. Jack Hart, who had been permitted to come into the dressing-room, reached over and gripped the younger man's shoulder hard.

He whispered, "Keep your chin up, son. Spike's outside and he's griping already because he's going to be out of a job."

Dan forced a smile. Then came the clipped, assured tones of the doctor as he prepared to remove the bandages. "Ready, Miss Austin?"

The crisp rustle of the nurse's uniform crackled stiffly beside Dan. "Yes, Doctor," the girl answered. "Are the lights subdued enough, do you think?"

"I believe so. All right, here we go. Take the heavy outer bandage off, please, Miss Austin."

Cool, light hands that moved with sureness tapped here and there around Dan's head. Sweat began to break out all over him, and the thought which had been pounding for days into his brain seemed to burn in flaming letters before him. "Maybe they've failed—maybe they've failed. Dear God, please, don't have let them fail."

He could tell by the release of pressure that the outer bandages had been removed. Then the doctor took charge, and the slow care with which he worked was maddening to Dan. Why couldn't he just rip them off and let him know once and for all what the answer was to be—life or continued blindness.

P

"Careful, Kirk," Dr. Howard advised. "Keep your eyes shut until I tell you to open them." Several minutes passed without a sound in the room but Dan's laboured breathing. The doctor spoke again. "Feel any pain? See any light?"

Dan shook his head. He was afraid to speak for fear his voice would crack.

Then he realised how foolishly he had anticipated the worst. "All right, then," the doctor said. "Now slowly, very slowly, draw your lids back. Open your eyes."

To Dan it seemed as though the skin of his forehead was being peeled back as he followed the doctor's instructions. While it was not painful, he had to exert real muscular effort to raise the long-bandaged lids. Suddenly pain did come—white blinding pain, and Dan stopped trying to open his eyes. He jerked instinctively as that white flash shot through his brain. Convulsively his hands clawed at the coverlet.

"It's no use, Doctor," he said hoarsely. "I guess you've done your best, but it's no use."

"Why do you say that, Kirk?" The doctor's voice carried a note of excitement.

Dan rubbed his damp forehead with the back of his hand. He shook his head. "The pain," he muttered. "A white, stabbing pain."

Dr. Howard spoke again, and this time he could not keep out the tone of exultation in his voice. "Pain? White—like a flash of light?" Dan nodded, ashamed of his weakness. "Then the operation was a success, my boy. That was light. You can see."

The next minute Hart was gripping Dan's shoulders, shaking him, and the nurse was wiping tears of joy from his cheeks. Dimly through the jumble of words of congratulation and encouragement Dan heard the doctor instructing the nurse. "Dark room for three full weeks. No excitement, and light bandage most of the time. Now, young fellow, we're going to take you to your room and let you rest."

But it was impossible for Dan to rest. The miracle of what had happened to him was too great to take in all at once, and as he lay in his bed, in the darkened room, his hand clutching Spike's thick fur, he spoke of it over and over again to Jack Hart, who sat beside him until the nurse gently shooed him away.

In the weeks that followed, Spike never left Dan's room except to be taken for an occasional airing by Hart. Gradually Dan was allowed to expose his eyes without a bandage for short periods each day, and gradually his eyes became stronger and he could move around the room unaided.

Spike's reaction to his master's sudden freedom of movement was laughable. Dan still wore his dark glasses, and of course, to the dog he was still in need of being led. The first time Kirk tried to walk unaided, he went from the bed to a table near the door. At Dan's first step, Spike leaped to his feet and stood directly in front of his master. Intent on what he was doing, Dan forgot for a moment that the dog had been laboriously trained to look out for him, and he casually stepped around him. Spike barked and leaped in front of him again. As Dan

continued to walk, Spike's whines and prancing
became frantic.

"I'll be blamed!" Dan said at last, finally realising
that the dog was hurt because he had moved without his aid. "You don't know I'm all right, do you,
old fellow?" He leaned over and held the dog's head
between his hands, shaking it from side to side.
Spike continued to whimper. "All right, all right,
when we get out of here I'll pretend you're leading
me till we get used to being normal again."

Spike's answer was to run to a chair in the corner,
grip the harness in his mouth, and drag it across the
floor to the bed. Then he lay down beside it and
looked up at Dan.

"I can see we'll have to take it easy breaking the
news to you, old boy . . . You've been the best pal
a man ever had, haven't you? Yes, you have," Dan
continued shaking the dog's head up and down in
an assenting motion. "I'll make it up to you yet,
you'll see."

As if to affirm the fact that his master's presence
was enough joy for him, Spike shook his head loose
and gave vent to a sharp, short bark.

Dan's recovery was rapid, but on the doctor's suggestion he stayed on at the hospital for some weeks.
He had a room on the first floor of the building,
with french windows leading directly into a garden
court. In the evenings, when the sun sank below the
surrounding tall buildings, Dan would attach Spike's
harness and walk for an hour or so in the garden.
It was his first chance to observe the dog's ability as
a leader, and Dan took delight in walking off the

path and making Spike take him in and out of the shrubbery. Whenever Spike tried to take a detour around bushes that Dan could not have formerly passed through, Dan corrected him by pressure on the harness. This way he hoped to make the dog realise that he was capable of doing some things for himself. At first this puzzled the dog, and he would look up over his shoulder at the man. Yes, he was the same, the same dark glasses and all—but he seemed to know where he was going. But he rapidly adjusted himself to these minor changes in his master.

Hart came in one evening while the two were out on their walk. "Hey, young fellow," he called from the doorway. "What's the big idea. You don't need Spike any more. Why don't you give him a well-earned rest."

Dan grinned. "Easier said than done. He wants to coddle me every time I move." He told Hart about the dog's resentment the first day he walked alone, and of Spike's bringing the harness to his bed. "So you see I haven't got the heart to let him know he's just a pet, not a working dog any more."

"You'll have to do it some day, Dan," Hart countered, "and it may as well be now. Seems kind of cruel to me, kidding him that way."

For a minute Dan was silent. "You'll be going back to the camps in a week or so?"

Hart nodded. "Sooner than that. I was planning on going back to-morrow."

"Nothing new about Great Western?" Dan inquired, looking quickly at Hart then away again.

"No-o-o," Hart drawled. "And I don't think they'll have the guts to start anything this season."

"Maybe," Dan answered cynically. "Whatever happened to that case against McQuade and Healy and the gang?"

Hart pursed his lips into a bitter line. "Nothing, blast it. Not a blamed thing. Healy and the rest are still out on bail and the trial's no nearer than it was before. Great Western's moving heaven and earth to have it thrown out of court, but I don't see how they can do that. Lucky for us these magistrates aren't downright crooked like those who handled your dad's case—just a wee bit anxious to put their hands on some hard cash."

"I'm not going to tell you now and I don't want you to ask me," Dan said, "but I'm not pulling the wool over Spike's eyes just to be mean. I've got a plan. Great Western headquarters are here, aren't they?"

"That's right."

"And Schwartz—is he in town, do you know?"

Hart nodded. "I saw his fat face in the paper just the other day. Some committee he's on is finishing up their work before Mr. Schwartz goes north to his hunting-lodge. Why? What's this all about?"

"Remember, no questions yet." Dan replied, grinning. "Could you put off going West till Friday?"

"Well . . ."

"If I come with you?"

"That's different. Sure. Why not?"

"I can leave the hospital on Friday, and we can go back together—that is, if you still want me to work for you."

Hart, laughing, stood up and for a reply hit the big fellow on the shoulder with his fist. "Do I! We'll tear up those sticks like our friend Paul Bunyan. Okay, Dan, see you on Friday."

For the rest of the week Dan kept pretty close to his room. He spent most of his time sitting in a chair by the french windows, a pad of yellow paper (since the doctor said that was the easiest on his eyes) on his knee, chewing the stub of a pencil. He would write feverishly for fifteen minutes or so, then tear the sheet and throw it away. Finally he had ten largely written sheets; satisfied, he tore the sheets from the pad and put them in a portfolio.

Friday came. Completely dressed, Dan nervously paced the room until it was time for Hart to show up. As he said good-bye to Dr. Howard, he pointed to Spike and said, "I don't have a leash for him, so I'd better keep the harness on. He's too good a dog to be run over by some wild Chicago driver."

Dr. Howard shook his hand and walked to the door with Dan. "You're right, Kirk, don't let anything happen to that fellow. And take care of yourself too. If you're ever in town drop in and look us over. Not that you'll be needing it. You're fit as a fiddle now."

In the taxicab speeding to the station, Hart asked, "What's the idea? Dark glasses and Spike in harness?"

Dan put his hand on Hart's knee before he spoke. "That's part of the plan I told you about. As far as you know, remember I'm still blind."

"Okay, you're the boss. Only," he added laughing,

"it hardly seems like proper gratitude after getting you the best eye specialist in town, a room in the best hospital, then you come out completely cured and act like this."

"Seriously, though, Jack. I don't know how to thank you. How on earth you ever——"

"Forget it, son. Nothing's good enough for Jim Kirk's boy—not that he's not pretty good on his own hook." There was a twinkle in Hart's eye.

"Okay, But why did you ever go to Howard?"

"Well," Hart answered slowly, "there's not a better medico in the world than old Doc Carrol—as far as accidents and ordinary sicknesses go. But I'll bet you that old geezer hasn't been to town in over ten years. And he probably hasn't read a medical book for fifty years. It didn't seem right, either, that you should go on having headaches. Then I heard of Howard—he was a surgeon during the World War and he knows his stuff—and, well, here we are."

The taxi sped north along the Outer Drive. Too moved to trust himself to speak, Dan kept his eyes glued on the window, soaking up the colours that were so bright they hurt. The pale blue of the sky, the deep blue of the water inshore, the dull grey blocks of stone piled on the water-washed sparkling beaches, the red brick of the apartment houses as they soaked up gold from the afternoon sun, and the flashing of innumerable windows. "Gosh, Jack," he exclaimed suddenly. "What a release it is! I can see, man. *See!* Do you understand that? Lord, but it feels good just to be alive!"

Hart laughed. "Sure, son. I think I know how you feel."

As they walked down the striated white marble steps to the waiting-room below, Dan noticed the admiring glances of passers-by, watching the dog steer him through the revolving doors, down the lengthy steps, and in and out of little knots of people.

They had a compartment in the middle of one of the long, modernistic coaches. The conductor had no objection to Spike's riding with the men, so he crawled between Dan and the window and kept his nose pushed against the glass, smearing it thoroughly. Staring out at the refineries, the grain elevators, dirty streets, and the gaunt backs of dingy apartment houses, Dan turned away and said to Hart, "Thank God we'll soon be out where there are some trees and hills and a lot of honest dirt."

Hart agreed with him. "It's not a pretty sight, is it? Neither are the woods when some of these gyppo outfits get through with them. We've got to keep our end up whether we live in the city or the country. Nature isn't going to wash streets and plant gardens any more than she'll reforest a timber stand when it's been cut close."

For a long time neither man said a word as the long train gradually left the last of the filling stations and hamburger stands behind and roared into the flat, open country where golden rows of corn rolled and waved in the wind.

They could not see the sunset clearly, for the train was heading directly west, but Dan thought that the subdued yet greyish mixture of blues, purples, reds and gold that came into his vision was the most gorgeous he had ever seen. For the first time in his life he was beginning to really see colours. When the sun reached the horizon and the bluish-purple clouds hovered over the reddish-coral afterglow, the tears came into his eyes and he had to turn his head away from the window and keep his eyes focused inside the car.

When it was quite dark outside, Hart turned to Dan and said, "Shall we go ahead to the diner or shall we have dinner in here?"

"Let's wait awhile," Dan said, taking his pipe out of his pouch and thoughtfully filling it. "You know, Jack," he continued, "I think we made a mistake."

"What do you mean?"

"Well, back there in Swift River I had a lot of crazy ideas floating around in my head, but it's only in the last couple of weeks that I've begun to see sense. You know all along we could get the connection between McQuade, Healy, and the rest and Great Western, but we haven't been regarding Great Western in the proper light."

"That sounds screwy to me. Say it over again."

"Well, who is Great Western?"

"You don't mean who—you mean what."

"No, I mean who. Great Western's just a holding company for a lot of little companies—like Dad's, for instance. As a company Great Western's probably no more innocent or guilty then the rest of us. What we've overlooked is the fact that the guiding light, and probably the evil light since

perty and reconsider the price. Will he come? As sure as my name's Dan Kirk. Why? First of all he's on his way to the hunting-lodge anyway; second, by condescending to come in person he can knock the price down some more. Oh, don't bother, he'll come."

Hart looked carefully at Kirk for a moment. "Dan, if I didn't know you so well I'd say you'd make a better pirate than J.P. himself. Frankly, although I couldn't admit it before, I was worried about what might happen this season. We might not be so lucky this time. Even if I am sticking my neck out on those letters, I'm with you. If I can't trust Dan Kirk, I can't trust any one."

"Then we're conspirators?" Dan asked.

Hart nodded, smiling. "The best ever. Shake on it."

Solemnly they shook hands, then Dan said, "Now let's eat."

They awoke Spike, who yawned and got into his harness, and walked forward to the dining-car.

Dan's homecoming was just a little disappointing to his three friends. Gathered down by the station to meet the train, their faces dropped when instead of a sprightly, healthful young fellow they saw Spike, who was still in harness, appear at the top of the steps, followed by Dan in dark glasses holding on to the harness. Dismally they shook hands and welcomed him back, but no one said much as they walked slowly towards Martin's cabin. Once inside the door, Dan took off the dark glasses, and looking at Rusty said, "My, that's a bright tie you have on."

Immediately pandemonium broke loose, and in a minute Dan's back was sore from the pounding it received. Rufe turned away and wiped his eyes, but Jerry frankly unashamed, let the tears roll down her cheeks.

Before leaving with Hart, Dan swore them all to secrecy, but the two men and the girl decided to hold an impromptu celebration anyway. The gala affair they planned, however, ended in dismal failure for the two men did not return to Martin's cabin till ten o'clock that night.

Bright and early next morning, dressed in her old overalls, high boots and a heavy sweater, Jerry trotted down the path to Dan's cabin. For the past week she had heard the insolent evening bobwhite of a covey of quail in the meadow beyond the tracks, and she thought that this morning might be a good time for investigating. But there was no response to her knock, and pushing open the door she discovered the cabin empty and the bed already made. Slowly kicking up the dust and stones, she walked back to the centre of town to her father's cabin. Yes, there they were, their heads huddled together over some papers and Spike snoozing very peacefully under Dan's chair.

Hearing her footsteps, Dan looked up. Hart's gaze followed Dan's. "Hello, girl," he said. "What gets you up so early?"

Lamely, realising her cause was hopeless, she said, "Oh, I thought maybe Dan would want to go gunning again."

Dan smiled, seeing the hurt in her eyes, and said, "Don't worry, Jerry, give us just a week or so and we'll have all the time in the world for that."

Pouting, she replied, "But I haven't all got the time in the world."

"Enough anyway," her father said. "Come on, wipe that mad look off your face and smile. That's right. . . . See you at lunch, honey."

Before Jerry had turned to go they had buried their heads in the papers. Gloomily she returned to Rusty's cabin, got her fishing pole, and went on down to the river.

For a week Dan and Hart anxiously awaited a reply to the letter Hart had written on company stationery and mailed when they got off the luxurious trans-continental train to transfer to the dirty local that brought them to Swift River. Letters were usually delivered every four days, and Hart spent the intervening time taking the rough drafts that Dan had prepared, to the company lawyer to put into legal language, and having a typist make copies of these agreements. Having nothing particular to do in all this time, Dan feverishly went over his plans and reread the drafts till his head split. As far as he could tell his scheme was foolproof—but the trout had not yet risen to the bait.

Hart had just returned from one of his trips to the county seat when Rufe brought him a letter that came on the evening train. It was beautifully typed on good paper, and in the upper left-hand corner of the envelope was the gothic return address of Great Western Lumber Company.

Quickly Hart tore the envelope from cover to cover. Reading over his shoulder, Dan laughed. "It's working out," he said. The letter repeated the offer Schwartz had made the year before, only now the sum he mentioned was lighter by some ten thousand dollars.

"He's a cool customer," Dan said. "He's in a pickle but does he ante his bid? Not him, he lowers it. You've got to give the fellow credit for brassy nerve."

Immediately Hart signed the reply that had been prepared beforehand, and it was sent by the morning train. There was nothing to do now but sit and wait.

In a week another massive envelope arrived. The letter inside contained words to the effect that since Mr. Schwartz was on his way to his hunting-lodge he would graciously grant Mr. Hart a day of his time.

Kirk and Hart read the letter over twice before they could believe it. Dan leaped and chuckled with glee. "He swallowed the bait, hook, line and sinker. We've got him, Jack! We've got him!"

Hart grinned, but his answer was sober enough. "Don't count your chickens before they're hatched. He hasn't signed anything yet."

"Hasn't signed anything! Man, when he put his name on that letter he signed his death warrant!"

In the next few days, between the receipt of the letter and the day of Schwartz's expected arrival, Hart selected half a dozen men from the road gang and brought them one at a time to headquarters, where they were interviewed carefully by Dan.

Most of the men interviewed had been in Camp Three at the time Healy had started his cut-off drive. Kirk explained enough of his plan to make it clear to the men what their duty would be, and when they found that their main task was to remove Healy, McQuade, and Read from the county seat to Camp One, their eyes lit up and they expressed no reluctance to do Dan's bidding. Their only question was why Dan couldn't see fit to bring the whole gang in. "Remember," Dan cautioned each man, "you're not to speak to any one else about this, not even your best buddy."

The afternoon of the day before Schwartz was expected to arrive, the chosen men filed into the big front-room office.

"You all know why you're here," Dan began, looking at the tense eager faces stretched up at him. "Any one not know?" Dan asked, pausing; but no one answered. "Good. Doyle will be your leader. He's the only one who knows all the men by sight. Remember, no settling of private grudges. We want those chaps here, but we want them here in good condition. Of course I have no objections to a black eye or so," he continued, laughing, and the men smiled with him. "But no hospital cases. Any questions? No? All right, then, snap to it. I don't have to impress on you the importance of keeping out of trouble with anyone in town but the men you have to get. And make sure not more than two of you are seen together at one time."

Silently the men filed out of the building into the two waiting trucks, and in a few minutes nothing was to be seen of the trucks but a cloud of dust near the ridge in the distance.

Turning to Hart, Dan said, "I feel like Wellington before Waterloo."

"Well, I always heard that generals who had the courage of their convictions were the best," Hart replied. "Here's hoping to-morrow won't be our Waterloo."

Late that night Dan Kirk lay on the cot in his cabin, fully clothed. He was too excited to worry about falling asleep, his ears full of the faint night sounds, straining to hear the return of the trucks. Suddenly, so far in the distance that it merged with the croaking of the bullfrogs, Dan heard the sound he was waiting for—the faint, pulsating throb of a gasoline engine. He got up, put on his shoes and windbreaker, and called Spike to him.

By the time the man and the dog reached Hart's cabin, the camp boss came out of the front door, zipping up his jacket. The headlights of the first truck approached and the two men waved them on up the road to Camp One. The second truck slowed down to pick them up, and they hopped on the running board, pushing the dog in the front seat. "All present and accounted for," Doyle said. "Got all three of them."

Too cold to speak, now that the truck had resumed speed, Dan nodded happily. So far it was an auspicious beginning.

The lighted windows of the mess hall at Camp One blazed out strangely in the early morning darkness. On one side of the room, cowering together on a bench were three men, watched over by the husky Doyle and other members of the road gang. Holding one hand on Spike's harness, Dan walked into the mess hall. He marched into the centre of the room, standing there for a full five minutes before he said a word. The men looked up when he came into the room, and one of them shuddered— Dan thought it was McQuade. The longer Dan stood the quieter and more uneasy the men became.

"Big Jim! Healy!" Dan suddenly called out in a loud voice. "Come here."

Shuffling, hating to come forward yet not daring to refuse, Big Jim Healy moved towards Dan.

"Stand in front of me, Healy," Dan commanded. He smiled—a cruel smile that had no warmth to it. "How do you like your handiwork? How does it feel to make a man blind?"

Healy's eyes went icy with fear, then he bent his head and looked at the floor.

"Come closer, Healy, so I can touch you." Healy shuffled closer to that fearful, unseeing figure.

"So you're not sorry? You'd do anything you were paid to do, eh? Well, I guess it's my business to make you sorry. . . ." Dan touched the point of his chin with his finger. "Hit me there, Healy. Come on, you're not afraid to hit a blind man, are you?" Nervously Healy tried to back away, and Dan said, "Do you want the boys to give you a working over?"

Finally Healy found the strength to mutter, "Not with that dog to rush me, I ain't."

Dan beckoned to Hart, who came forward and took Spike away.

"Okay, now you're not afraid, are you, Big Jim?"

The taunt got under Healy's skin. His mouth tightened in a snarl and without warning his fist shot out at Dan's chin. Easily, simply, Dan moved his head back and to one side, and the haymaker sailed harmlessly over his shoulder. Before Healy realised what had happened, Dan's right flicked out and caught Healy on the side of the jaw, sending him sprawling ten feet away on the floor. He sat there, shaking his head from side to side, feeling his jaw, a dazed look in his eyes.

Dan stood quietly for a moment. The other two looked from Healy outstretched on the floor back to Dan. Kirk noticed with satisfaction that they were perspiring.

Finally Dan spoke. "I hope you boys get the point. We're through fooling with you. We mean business and we're going to sweat the truth out of you if we keep you here till you rot. . . . Take a look around," Dan said, gesturing to the members of the road gang who were acting as guards. "These are the men you nearly killed by that drive." Dan chuckled, but to the listening men the chuckle was anything but a comforting sound. "We know who hired you— Schwartz of Great Western. Unfortunately for you, Schwartz had the trial put off for some time, got you bail, so nobody's going to miss you for quite a while. Schwartz will probably say good riddance. And here you fellows are.

"Now, men, I've got a little proposition to talk over with you, but first of all I want you to take some time to think it over. You may as well stand up. You can think better on your feet. Any one of you three who makes a break or tries to sit down will be given a ducking. There's no heat in here and I don't need to tell you how easy it is to catch pneumonia."

Dan and Hart left, and Doyle, first staggering the captives so that they stood five feet away from any of the walls and out of easy reach of one another, passed out two typewritten sheets to the three men. The first of these sheets was an unconditional confession of complicity in the attempt to ruin Northern, naming Schwartz as the instigator. The second was the guarantee of Northern Lumber Company, signed by Hart and Kirk, that if they confessed their part in the plot the case against them would be let drop and that each man would be hired by Northern for a period of at least one year at the prevalent rate of wages.

Nervously Hart and Kirk stood at the station awaiting the express that would bring J. P. Schwartz to Swift River. Dan still wore his dark glasses, and he held Spike's harness nervously in his left hand. The dog felt some of his master's uneasiness; instead of sitting quietly by Dan's side, he pranced around and took little steps first to one side then the other. Despite the fact he had not slept in over a day—twenty-eight hours to be exact—Dan felt fit and fresh. He smelled deeply of the cool morning air with appreciation, and the warmth of the sun on his back brought a welcome sense of well-being.

They had been standing at the station only fifteen minutes or so when the rails began to sing. Looking up the tracks, they could see the smoke from the express streaming over the trees in the distance; and in a minute the train was upon them, wheels screaming, the brakes showering sparks. The engineer overshot the station again.

Hart, who had changed into a business suit and a felt hat, turned and smiled at Dan. "Here comes our fish," he said. Dan gave him a sickly smile in return and stood watching as Hart ran on down the tracks to meet Schwartz. The man was a long time getting off the train. First a coloured porter descended, carrying a yellow stool under his arm which he placed beneath the bottom step. He waited while half a dozen tan-coloured bags and two brief cases were handed down to him. Finally the great man himself appeared. Schwartz wore a dark blue hat, a dark grey suit with a pink pin stripe in it, grey gloves, and black and white striped tie with a diamond stickpin. The conservative clothes could not hide the fact that he had become much stouter and flabbier in the year or more since Dan had last seen him.

Hart introduced Dan as his "helper." Purposely Dan failed to find Schwartz's hand when it was offered; when he did shake it, the flesh was soft and damp. "Fish is right," he said to himself, wiping his hand surreptitiously on the side of his trousers.

"Suppose I check in at the hotel before we discuss business, Mr. Hart," Schwartz said when the introductions were over.

Hart laughed and waved his hand in the direction of the low one and two story cabins that made up the village of Swift River. "Do you see anything there that looks like a hotel, Mr Schwartz? Don't worry, we'll make you comfortable."

"What about my baggage," Schwartz persisted, fingering his tie.

"I'll have some one pick it up later. Just leave it here for the present," Hart said easily.

On their way to the truck, Hart whispered to Schwartz, "I hope you don't mind the young fellow. He got hurt in an accident and we let him tag along, to make him feel good."

"Not at all, not at all," Schwartz replied, surprise evident in his round little eyes.

It was not until Schwartz found that he was going to have to make his tour of inspection in a truck that his sudden dissatisfaction crystallised. He had had a good breakfast that morning, and was feeling particularly good, so good that he decided he would not try to beat down the first price he had quoted Northern. But when Spike got in the truck and sat between Dan's knees, and Hart started the truck with a jerk, pressing the gear shift back into his thigh, Schwartz's mounting dissatisfaction reached a peak. Daintily plucking a dog hair from his immaculate suit, he suddenly resolved to get Northern for not a penny more than his first offer minus ten thousand. Having reached this conclusion, he leaned back and paid a little attention to what Hart was telling him about the roads and the tractors. They passed the road gang, stripped to the waist, hard at work on the new road, and in three-quarters of an hour were at Camp One. By that time Schwartz's price was fifteen thousand less.

Hart stopped the truck in front of the mess hall and excused himself to get some papers and maps. "Take a look around; Mr. Kirk will keep you company," he told Schwartz.

Gingerly, carefully stepping over obstacles that might scuff up his expensive shoes. Schwartz followed Dan around the camp, slowly becoming more and more enraged. He had not come up here to be lectured at, he told himself. Besides it had been a long time since he had visited a logging camp, and the squalour of it all, or what seemed to him to be squalour, weighed on his spirits, until he began silently cursing the judgment that had brought him to come to this place.

As they stood in front of the blacksmith shanty, Schwartz stopped mopping his brow long enough to remark bitterly to Dan, "You get around spry enough for a fellow who—who can't see so well."

"Oh, that," Dan replied laughing. "You get used to it. I know this place by heart. We had a jam up on the Swift this spring. In trying to break it I got hit on the head. Ruined the optic nerve. . . . Funny thing," he continued, "you own that property north of the Cranmer, don't you?"

"Why, yes, yes I do," Schwartz stuttered, surprised.

"Somehow a foreign gang got up on your property and started a drive to jam us here. If it hadn't been for that I'd have my sight. God, what wouldn't I do to get my hands on the guy that started it!"

Dan clenched his hands so tightly that his knuckles showed white.

"Yes, yes," Schwartz said nervously. "I guess so."

Just then, by a prearranged plan, the door of the blacksmith shop opened and young Doyle walked out with Wes Read in tow. Narrowly watching Schwartz, Dan saw the man start suddenly, his flushed skin turning white.

"Who—who are those men?" he asked Dan.

"What? What men?"

"Oh. I'm sorry, you can't see them, can you? Just two men. I wondered who they were," he said, breathing easier now that the two had disappeared between the buildings without Read having given any sign of recognition.

"I really don't know," Dan said. "Lots of new men this year. Hart picked them up somewhere. Let's go on."

"What's keeping Hart, I wonder?"

Not deigning to answer, Dan shook Spike's harness, and the dog set off at a rapid pace that soon brought them to the edge of the Swift. On the way Dan pointed out the convenient arrangement of the stock piles. Standing on the bank of the river—full again after the drying summer months—Dan had to shout to make himself heard above the noise of its rush.

"Don't you think we'd better be getting back?" Schwartz shouted.

Dan shook his head. "Not yet. Beautiful sight, isn't it? Yet a man could easily lose his life in there. Desolate country around here, too. Put a man across in those woods without an axe or a canoe and he'd never come back. Probably starve to death. I know. Spent all winter in them. Never see a soul."

All the time he was chattering Dan kept one eye on Schwartz. The big fellow pulled back a spotless cuff and looked at the platinum watch on his wrist. Evidently he didn't care over much for this spot.

"You're not nervous, are you, Schwartz?" Subtly Dan's tone had changed, and the man looked up at him indignantly. Schwartz suddenly felt but one desire—to get out of this place and go on to his hunting-lodge.

"I can't spend all day here—where's your boss?" he said, turning around towards camp.

"Just a minute." Dan's hand reached out and grasped Schwartz's upper arm in a vicelike grip.

Schwartz's face flushed. With his free hand he took hold of Dan's wrist and tried to pull the hand away. "Here, take your hand away, fellow. This is ridiculous behaviour. Idiotic. I'll report you to Hart. Who are you, anyway?"

"I'm glad you asked that question, Schwartz. Did you ever hear of the Kirk Lumber Company?"

"Of course. I control it."

"That's right—how stupid of me! Then you remember Mr. James Kirk, the former owner?"

"Yes, yes. Kirk's claims were faulty. We bought him out and he fought us. We beat him in court. What the devil is all this? I didn't——" Twisting, he tried to break loose from Kirk's grip.

"Don't try that again, or I'll break your arm," Dan said quietly. He was beginning to enjoy the fellow's discomfiture. Sweat poured down his forehead despite the cool breeze near the river. "And this Mr. Kirk—he died, didn't he?"

"I believe so. That's no concern of mine."

"On the contrary—it's very much your concern. And mine. You see, Schwartz, I happen to be Dan Kirk—James Kirk's son." Schwartz looked wildly around for some means of escape. "I wouldn't try running—or shouting either. There's no one around to hear you and Spike here'd bring you down in ten feet."

"I—I," Schwartz sputtered. "I won't stand for any more of this impertinence. I'm going to see Hart."

"That's a good idea," Dan said calmly. "I'll go with you."

Schwartz stopped short in his mad rush into Hart's cabin. In a chair facing the door, imperturbably smoking a pipe, sat Hart. He looked up calmly at the purple and flustered Schwartz.

"Look here——" Schwartz began, but he stopped short when he saw the look of utter contempt fleeting across Hart's face.

"Sit down," Hart said, pushing a paper over the table towards the now greatly flustered tycoon. "Better sign that."

Schwartz did not even look at the paper. "See here. I came up to this god-forsaken place at your invitation to look over a piece of property that——"

Hart knocked out his pipe on the edge of the table; the noise was so loud it drowned out whatever Schwartz was gong to say. "What do you take us for, Schwartz—babes in the woods? Did you honestly think we'd sell this property for a song—just so you could develop that land up north? I thought you had a good business head. We'll give you three minutes to sign that paper."

Schwartz started to rise. Dan reached over and pushed him down in the chair again. "Do as Mr. Hart says—sign that paper."

Schwartz picked up the paper and glanced quickly through it. In legal language it stated simply that former employees of Great Western Lumber had out of spite started the drive on Northern in order to implicate Great Western, and that therefore these employees—naming them—were guilty of causing untold property damage and should bear the costs of charges and damages.

"This is an outrage!"

"Better sign it," Dan advised nonchalantly.

"And if I refuse?"

Dan shrugged his shoulders. "You saw the river —did it look inviting? It would make a nice story for the newspapers, wouldn't it? 'Mr. Schwartz dies in sight of rescuers. The well-known business tycoon, on a business trip . . . etcetera, etcetera!' You put in the gory details."

Scwartz thought quickly. He smiled to himself. His mistake had been in neglecting to take into consideration the human factor; too long he had been making schemes and making men fit those schemes like pawns in a game of chess. He realised that now. He had forgotten how totally unlike pawns human beings could act, and sometimes their actions were devilish inconvenient to a man like himself. But he smiled to himself. He was getting off easy. That fool Hart! "Thought you had a good business head." He had if this was all they were getting out of him. Besides the signature could probably be proved invalid later.

"Do you have a pen?" He asked Hart.

Hart dried the wet ink by waving the paper, then, reached over and put on his hat. He said to Dan, "I'll be back in a minute. Keep our friend occupied."

Inside of ten minutes Hart was back. Whistling as he came through the door, he dropped a sheaf of papers in front of Dan—the signed confessions. Dan grinned up at the camp boss, whose eyes sparkled. "All of them?" Dan asked.

"All of them."

Kirk took the top signed confession from the pile—it was Healy's—and handed the paper to Schwartz. "You'll find that rather interesting, Mr. Schwartz."

If Schwartz's face had been purple before it was a mild purple compared to the colour that made his face livid now. His collar suddenly ceased attempting to look starched and wilted in front of their eyes. Pounding the table, Schwartz shouted, "It's a lie. This is the most preposterous—Why, you two are the dirtiest crooks——" He sputtered so that he could not say another word.

Hart and Kirk laughed; then, just as suddenly as he started to laugh, Dan lost his temper. Bending over, he seized Schwartz by the lapel of his suit and shook him as a terrier shakes a rat. He took off his dark glasses and threw them in the corner of the room. "You dirty murderer! I'm the man you nearly blinded, Schwartz. Thank God for Hart here and medical science it didn't quite happen, but it would be all the same to you if it did or not. I'm Jim Kirk's son, Schwartz—think of that! You killed him just as coldbloodedly as though you'd gone after him with a knife. Why, I've a——"

Hart held Dan's upraised arm in a strong but gentle grip. "Easy, son, easy." Dan quieted immediately, slumping down in his chair, his face flushed, his heart pounding. Hart turned towards Schwartz.

"We're through playing, Schwartz. We know as well as you do that it was you who hired those men to start that jam so you could drive us out of business and save your own neck. We know it was you who furnished the money to have Dan's father's claims proved faulty. These confessions prove it. And we're through playing with local judges and lawyers who can be bought, Schwartz. How would it sound to you to have the federal government look over this stuff?" Hart pointed to the confessions on the table. "Frankly this is the only dirty deal we have proof of, but the federal government has an uncanny knack of finding those things out. You're licked, Schwartz, and you know it. If you want to save your skin at all, you had better do what we say."

Jack Hart turned and pointed out of the window. Outside the three captives of the night before, who had been released now that they had signed the confession, were walking around the yard smoking and stretching. He turned back to Schwartz. "Do you think those fellows would show you any mercy if we turned you loose among them?"

"What do you want?" Schwartz asked finally.

"Just two things. First a resignation and complete transfer of the Kirk property to the son, Dan Kirk, for services rendered. Second, a transfer of that Cranmer property to Northern Lumber Company in full payment for damages sustained. We have the papers here—all you have to do is sign them."

Thinking of his own skin still, Schwartz asked, "How do I know if I sign these, you won't go to the federal government anyway?"

"You'll have to take our word for that, Schwartz. You're hardly in a position to dictate."

Schwartz signed.

"How soon can I get out of here?" he croaked.

Dan spoke up. "Right away. First you'll have to take a little trip to the county seat to have these agreements recorded. And I'll keep these confessions here until I hear definitely from Hart that that's been done." Dan turned to Hart. "Do you mind if young Doyle goes with you instead of me? I think I'll take the afternoon off and go gunning."

Hart grinned. "Not at all, son. If we were near a drugstore, I'd buy you a chocolate soda."

Dan and Hart shook hands before Hart jumped in the truck and sat down beside Schwartz. "Confidentially," Dan said in a whisper, "how did you ever get those fellows to sign?"

"It was easy. Just let them see the paper Schwartz signed. It was no trouble at all."

"Well, partner——"

"Partner?"

"Yes, wouldn't you like to go into partnership with Kirk and Son?"

Hart looked at Dan straight in the eyes, then grinned. "Yes. Shake—partner."

Dan watched until the truck disappeared from view behind a clump of trees. Then he bent over and engaged Spike in a wrestling match. For a minute nothing was to be seen but dust and fur and an occasional portion of man. They unscrambled, and Dan hugged the big dog to him. "How are you, Spike, you old scoundrel? Shall we take a walk! Come on, speak!"

Spike waved his tail and his body until it looked as though he would shake himself apart. He barked.

"Or shall we get Jerry and go hunting?" Dan asked. "Speak! Come on, boy, speak!"

Spike wagged his tail some more, then stood up with his paws on the man's shoulder and barked twice in his master's face.

"So be it, then. Let's go."

Man and dog trotted down the dusty road together.

THE END